HOUSE OF SIN

LACY DANES

HOUSE OF SIN

Her most important duty—serve the master's pleasure.

Emily's dreams are simple: a life of dedicated service at a respectable estate, and a strong marriage filled with love and devotion for one man. Portage Place, the manor where her parents apprenticed, seems the perfect place to start. Though it is whispered that all is not as it seems behind its grand façade.

The rumors, it turns out, ring with truth. The halls are saturated with sensuality, desire and lust. Despite the scandalous duties she is asked to perform, she is determined not to stumble on what could be her first step toward her dreams. Dreams that, lately, have included the manor's fiery haired groomsman.

A promise to watch over his younger half-brother brought Adam to Portage Place. For the first time in five years of enjoying the delights of the manor's unbridled debauchery, Emily's innocence touches the protector that still lives deep in his core. This house of sin may have ruined him, but he will see to it that it doesn't ruin her.

It seems, however, that behind every door lurks a conspiracy to bind Emily in velvet chains of desire. Until the only way out is for Adam to take the biggest risk of all...

To my awesome 4novelistas gals Christina Crooks, Susan Lyons and Delilah Marvelle. Without you I would not have finished this story. You have been my strength and encouragement when things were not working right. I adore you.

To my dear friend Shelli Stevens for suggesting to publish this story. We have been friends through so much. You are an awesome, amazing friend and I am so happy I know you. Hugs.

CHAPTER 1

Cornwall England, 1879

The ancient butler who sat across the narrow wooden desk stared at her with harsh green eyes. His lips turned down and pursed, twitching the flesh in his oblong face. "Is this your first position, miss?"

"Y-yes, sir." Emily inwardly cringed. She should have kept her voice strong yet quiet as her mother had instructed when in the company of those she should respect, but she was nervous and the way that man kept looking at her gave her very little to respect.

She glanced at the doctor, who stood not two arms' lengths away. His fair hair and sideburns washed out the smooth, pale skin of his face. If it were not for his startling blue eyes he would have appeared an apparition. His eyes... She lowered her gaze to the stained whitewashed floor. His eyes captivated.

"Remove your chemise, miss," the doctor said in a calm and reassuring tone.

Her knees shook and her heart pounded. She didn't want

to remove her shift and expose her body for the doctor and butler to inspect. She swallowed hard. She would anyway, as houses of quality inspected their unwed female hires for virtue. It was a sign the servant would uphold the house's morals.

Her fingers grasped the thin fabric, and she lifted the cotton up and over her head. From all her mother had said, Mr. Waterton demanded respect in his household. She would obey him and his rules explicitly. Even if standing before him with nothing but her drawers, stockings and boots on was a bit alarming.

"You come from a good serving stock. Both your parents were employed by our late master and used those skills to enter grander establishments," Mr. Waterton stated in a flat tone.

Emily stood still and continually rubbed the tips of her fingers against her palm in an anxious gesture. Goosepins raced her skin as she glanced around the tiny, windowless room and swallowed hard. The space was cramped, and the heat from three bodies pressed in on her. Her head spun. She had fainted before in small spaces under less vexation. She inhaled a steadying breath. *Not now, Emily. This is too important for your prospects. No one hires inexperienced servants, and this is your only answered inquiry. It is this or begging your existence as a cock-chafer in the streets.*

"Please remove your drawers, miss." The doctor's intense blue gaze lowered down her body to the tapes that held her knickers in place.

Her drawers… The way his eyes lit when he looked at her… Distasteful. Her heart jumped against her breast, and she stared at him with wide eyes. *Do as he asks, Emily.* With shaking hands, she pulled the tapes about her knees and then the ones about her waist free. The white linen fell to the floor in a heap. She straightened her spine. One less bit of proper clothing to hide behind. She trembled and diverted her gaze to the same stained spot on the floor. When would this embarrassment end?

"You are doing fine, miss." The doctor's cold, smooth hand grasped her wrist.

Her muscles flinched. *Stay still, Emily.* His touch was as icy as the ghostly illusion she wished he could be.

His fingertips pressed to the underside, and he looked down at his etched silver pocket watch. His thick, golden hair fell in ringlets covering his stunning blue eyes.

Emily swallowed hard. Here she stood before an oddly striking man her own age as he inspected her as if she was a broodmare he wished to breed his stallion to. She inhaled a steadying breath. A mix of clean honey soap and eucalyptus waved as if mist between them. Oh, but he smelled good. *Stay focused on the task. You should be thinking of why this kind of scrutiny is necessary for a position as maid.* She was hired to clean the pots, for gracious sake. A hasty check of her virtue was all that was appropriate, even if a bit humiliating. This kind of inspection seemed inordinate.

"You shall follow Miss Lamber in her daily activities. Those activities shall include washing the linens, cleaning the pots and, when requested, doing anything the master, his sons, or guests ask of you. Is this understood, Miss Grey?" Mr. Waterton glared at her from the other side of the ever-shrinking desk.

She wanted this position in life. To serve. She had known this since birth. She would follow by her parents' example and find the fulfillment she craved in service. Yet she had no inkling what to expect here.

"Yes, sir." *Anything...* Emily nodded as the word buzzed around in her ears. She was good at following orders. However, what *anything* could entail raised all the hairs on her neck. Her brows pinched together as the doctor's fingers traveled up her arm to her neck. A ripple of goosepins followed in his wake, and her nipples tightened. Anything certainly included this monstrous scrutiny. This entire morning could easily pass as a fictional inspiration or a fantastical dream. Served her right for reading all those silly romance sheets about doctors and handsome rakes. Heaving bosoms and palpitating orbs. She glanced down at her pointed buds. Hers were anything but.

"Miss Grey." The doctor called her back calmly to reality. "Please sit back on the edge of the desk so I may inspect your..." His cheeks turned bright red, setting off the contrast of his piercing blue eyes. He cleared his throat. "Your nether regions."

Emily's eyes widened. Her nether regions? The check of her virtue and her worth as an unwed servant. She turned her head toward the butler, who continued to scribble a note on the very desk on which she was about to display herself. He didn't seem remotely out of sorts by the doctor's orders. This appeared to be his wish.

She swallowed hard. *Do as they request. This is what is required for the post.* She stepped backward until her bottom cheeks touched the edge of the cool desk. Her fingers gripped the curve of the carved edge, and she glanced back at the butler.

He continued to scribble on the parchment, unmoved by the closeness of her bare bottom.

Her hands trembled as she pushed her bottom up to do as

the doctor requested. She shivered as the cold, hard surface supported her rounded bum.

"Only a moment more, Miss Grey." The doctor stepped toward her with a reassuring smile. "Please scoot back a bit and put your heels on the edges so your legs are spread, miss."

Spread...

He wanted her to display her innocence to him. She closed her eyes, and her face blazed with heat that shot straight down her gut to the flesh between her thighs. She squirmed. It was not as if she was an unfortunate woman they were hiring as a favor. She was the daughter of two highly respected servants who Mr. Waterton had trained himself.

"Only a moment more, miss."

Did he feel repeating the short duration of her humiliation would somehow make it better? She pulled her legs up and out, placed the soles of her favorite pink boots on the ungiving wooden surface and squeezed her eyes closed tighter as her fantastical dream was about to turn nightmare. Her heart pounded and she held still. She displayed herself for a man other than a future husband.

A touch pressed to her thigh.

She trembled in unease and fear. No one besides herself had touched her there. Certainly the thought of a doctor's touch was less than impelling. No matter how differently striking he was, he was not the man she would wed. She bit her lip, and fever raced her skin. The flesh between her thighs tingled, and she fought the desire to close her legs on his hand.

His fingers glided through her hairs and parted her flesh, then slid into her.

She jerked and sucked in a startled breath. *Dear God! He entered me.* Was that the only way to check one's virtue?

In a rhythmic motion, the doctor's finger swirled around

inside her, then slid out. She let out a shaky breath. His hand touched her thigh once again, covered in moisture. "She is clean, Mr. Waterton."

"Clean?" The word escaped her before she could contain it.

"Thank you, Doctor Benson." The butler stood from the desk behind her and walked to the door.

Doctor Benson grabbed her shift from the desk and handed it to her. His blue eyes stared into hers. "I was checking for syphilis. You are clean and appear to be completely intact."

She swallowed. "No...I never...that is..."

"Miss Grey." He smiled at her. "You will do well here. I am around often and if you ever have any questions about your health or the way of things here, please come to me. I will do all I can to enlighten and protect you." His eyes narrowed as his fingers wrapped hers on the desk and squeezed a bit too harshly.

"You may put your legs down now, miss."

Her cheeks blazed with heat. He didn't have to say that again. Emily jumped off the desk as if the wood were possessed. She stood, pulled her shift over her head and grasped up her clothing.

Mr. Waterton reentered the small room. His lips formed a thin, straight line. Had he ever smiled a day in his life? He stared at them. "No need to dress, Miss Grey, as Miss Lamber will fetch your service attire." The butler tilted his head to the side and his gaze narrowed on her breasts.

Emily quickly pressed her clothes to her chest.

His lips turned down and then he glanced over his shoulder. "Miss Lamber, please enter."

A middle-aged woman with a heart-shaped face, crystal blue eyes and black hair pinned beneath a dark green cap entered. She wore an all-brown livery. Her plump lips curved into a cheery smile, and she bowed her head in respect. "Sir."

Emily's shoulders relaxed. She was no longer alone among the lewd men.

"Miss Grey will be under your tutelage." Mr. Waterton didn't look up and continued to write something on a piece of paper before him. "Please demonstrate all necessary to thrive and keep her position within this house."

"Yes, sir." The woman nodded.

"Get on with it." His voice was filled with displeasure. "There is much to accomplish this day, as the master's guest arrives shortly." He held out the parchment to Doctor Benson.

"Yes, sir." Emily bowed her head and followed Miss Lamber out of the small room into the long, narrow servants' hallway. She glanced back through the doorway and met Doctor Benson's sapphire eyes once more. *I will do all in my power to enlighten and protect you.* What was that supposed to mean?

"Don't fret over Mr. Waterton. He has been a fixture in this house for three generations," Miss Lamber called over her shoulder from up the hall.

Emily flinched, then scurried down the long, narrow white hall. Photographs of the servants hung lined up as if soldiers of the present. She wished she had time to stop and linger over the souls that had passed through this house. She wished such a thing had been present when her parents worked here. If only she could see their faces again.

"Though I don't think he much cares for our current master." The curves of Miss Lamber's hips swung back and forth as she ambled sensuously down the hall. "Mr. Waterton runs the best house in Cornwall. Ask any of the servants who work here at Portage Place. We are six menservants and six womanservants. All of us find this place home."

Wasn't it disrespectful for this woman to say Mr. Waterton did not like the current master? Though maybe he didn't like anyone at all.

Emily said not a word and simply followed Miss Lamber down the white-painted hall filled with grim faces and up a flight of equally narrow stairs.

"You will need to dress first. The master has strict rules for all the staff attire. I will also explain some things that are necessary and expected. Mr. Waterton is strict about taking precautions to ensure your longevity here as a servant."

"That is kind of him."

"Oh…so you do speak." She glanced over her shoulder and smiled. "Has nothing to do with being kind. If he loses you for any reason, he is out a trained servant and has to train a new. Which is most inconvenient."

They walked into a room tucked into the eaves, and Miss Lamber shut the door behind them. "You shall be sharing a room with me." The room was plainly dressed with grey walls and two small windows. The furnishings consisted of one bed, one table and one clothes closet. Though it was small, it was bigger than the room she'd had at Chesterfield Hall. She would be comfortable sleeping here. She simply hoped Miss Lamber was an easy sleeper, as the bed would indeed be cramped.

Miss Lamber walked to the scanty bed on the left side of the room. "Though we shall be sleeping together, the attire is yours alone." She held up the brown skirt and matching shirt that had lain upon the bed. "Get dressed."

Along with the brown attire was the same deep green cap that Miss Lamber wore. Emily grasped the brown skirt. The softest velvet fabric met her fingers. How odd. Why would anyone want their staff wearing something so expensive while doing chores? She ran the fabric down her belly and lifted her foot, eager to step into the soft creation.

"Oh, wait!"

Emily stilled.

Miss Lamber stepped forward with a blue ceramic bowl in her hand. "This part Mr. Waterton insists upon. I know it may be odd, but it truly does work. The good doctor told us how to do it." She thrust the bowl toward Emily.

Emily grasped the dish and glanced down into the ceramic vessel. Strips of cloth seeped in golden oil resided in the bowl. Why would Doctor Benson give them a bowl with oil and cloth? "What is this for?"

"For your protection, of course."

Emily's eyes widened on the bowl, then her gaze jumped to Miss Lamber's mischievous blue eyes. A biting unease flipped her gullet. "Protection from what?"

"You are to place one of these cloths up there, of course." Miss Lamber pointed to the slit in her knickers.

Emily's lips parted as her brows came together. *What?*

The corner of Miss Lamber's lip curved up and her cheek dimpled. "Then you won't end up leaving this place in less than a year…in the family way."

Emily stared at her in disbelief. "I beg your pardon, but I don't intend to accept advances from any man while I am in servitude. The mistress of the house would dismiss me flat out, and I require this position. I am not a strumpet and intend on waiting for marriage before I give in to that base desire."

Miss Lamber's brows pulled tight. "There is no mistress here. There is only the master and his sons. You do know about how a man and woman get on?"

Emily swallowed hard. Without a mistress, the entire house's morals could go wild. The doctor had checked her for syphilis... *You will get on well here,* assaulted her ears again. My gracious. Where she had simply thought him distasteful, he was entirely indecent!

Her parents had worked here under Mr. Waterton. They had never mentioned anything scandalous about this house. Surely she could keep her dream while working here. She was certain no matter how different Portage Place was, learning to be a good maid in this post would set her on a good path in life. She would gain experience. But what exactly did Miss Lamber mean? She needed to know more.

Emily's cheeks grew warm, and she swallowed hard. *Ask, Emily. Ask!* "Yes, of course I know about a diddle. B-but what does that have to do with working here?"

Miss Lamber's smile turned wicked. "The master has no vexation with the act and wishes it upon all of his servants and acquaintances. The art of pleasure is everywhere here and highly encouraged. There truly is no better place to work."

The act was encouraged here. Emily's throat closed off, and she swallowed hard. She closed her eyes. *...when requested, do anything the master, his sons, or guests ask of you.* Mr. Waterton's ominous words rang in her mind.

Anything.

Anything...

Including all acts of pleasure?

It couldn't be that debauched. She was letting her mind get the better of her. Besides, she needed this post. It was the only way to gain the experience she needed to be a servant. Surely she could figure a way to follow her dream of servitude and virtue here. She opened her eyes, realized her jaw was open, closed it, then licked her lips. "I—I—" They could not force her to accept an advance. Or could they?

"Here." Miss Lamber stepped toward her. "Let me place the cloth so you know how to do it right. As you follow me throughout the day, you shall see what I mean. I do think in time you will enjoy it here." She grasped the bowl back from Emily. "I will show you. Teach you. And please…call me Sibila."

"I am Emily." She hesitated and glanced around the room, not sure whether to flee in the horror her mind created or stay and see what this house was all about.

Sibila smiled at her. "Nice to meet you, Emily. Now pull up your shift and lie on our bed with your legs spread open so that I may place this."

It made little sense to give up a good post just because she feared what might be. Emily grasped the fabric that hung about her legs and pulled it up. This was shameful.

She sat on the bed. Her heart hammered, and the lips of her private place still tingled from the doctor's probing. She scooted back on the soft mattress and lay down. *Do this protection, and on the first scandalous advance, leave.* She could do that. Inching her legs up into a bent position, the soles of her shoes on the coverlet, she exposed her most private place to this woman she had met not an hour past. She swallowed hard. Blasphemous. Scandalous. Never would she have thought…

Concentrate on something else, Emily.

Her gaze darted around the tiny room. The small glass windows parted with a single wooden arch in each. The plain grey walls. The small mirror which hung above a stand with an equally plain white washbasin set atop it. Nothing caught her attention. The bed. She lay upon a bed exposed to a woman in a most humiliating way! *Shake those thoughts from your head. Concentrate on the bed if you must…the bed.*

The bed beneath her was covered in a thick white cotton coverlet. The mattress was plush and comfortable. Actually it appeared to be the most comfortable she had lain on. She wiggled her hips just a bit into the fluffy cradling of the pillow itself.

Sibila laughed and placed herself standing at the edge of the bed between her legs. "Getting comfortable, are we? Or are you bit of a naughty girl?" Her voice humored.

"I am attempting to distract myself."

"Ah, well, I am going to place it now. It will only be a moment more." Sibila's fingers touched her knee.

All the muscles in Emily's leg jumped. Why did everyone insist on telling her it would only be a moment more? No matter how short it was, it was an eternity.

"It will get easier each time. Before long, it will simply be part of your daily routine."

Sibila's fingers parted the folds of Emily's slit. "You are the virgin you said you were."

Emily squeezed her eyes tightly closed. "Yes."

"We shall keep that a confidence between you, me and the good doctor, or the master's sons will fight to be the first to bed you. You should choose who the first man will be. Not any one of them, as they are animals and think only with their wackers."

Sibila's finger slowly slid into her body, stretching her flesh. Emily sucked in a startled breath and gripped the bed linens.

"I am going to open you up a bit so I can slip this in easier." A drizzle of oil slid down between her legs, and Sibila's finger pressed in and out of her opening just as the doctor's had done.

She squirmed and pulled her buttocks away from the sensation. *Make haste.*

Sibila's touch glided out and up one lip of her privates, then circled and dipped back into her.

A fuzzy pressure stirred in her womb.

"There. Your muscles are relaxing. Doesn't that feel good?"

"Ummm…" It did feel…good. She should be mortified by such thoughts, such temptations.

"Simply concentrate on the pleasurable sensations. You should do this every time you feel the tingling sensation between your legs. Your body will so appreciate it." Her fingers continued to slide in and out and in and out, stretching the flesh of her slit wider and wider.

With each dip, a warm pleasure streamed through her and her muscles tightened. She held back a gasp and turned her head to the side as heat bloomed across her face. How embarrassing a sensation. Emily squirmed even more. This shouldn't feel good. Her hips arched as heat pulsed through her flesh.

"I am going to slide the cloth in now." Thick, cool wetness pressed to the slit of her opening, and then two fingers slid the cloth up and inside of her. "All is done."

Emily opened her eyes and blinked. Gracious. Pushing up with her hands, she sat upright, the flesh between her thighs throbbing. Thank goodness. "Do I need to worry about the strip slipping out?"

"No. At the end of each day, you will pull it out, and in the morning place another."

Emily nodded. Part of her daily routine? Wasn't touching yourself daily a sin and bad for your health? She glanced at Sibila. Her ruddy cheeks and energizing presence put her in the picture of health. There appeared to be no ill effect. Besides, protection was required if she was to stay on here.

"First duty is the master's chambers. Pull the sheets, fluff the mattress and clean the pots."

And then bed the master? *Truly, Emily, grasp hold of your imagination.*

CHAPTER 2

*E*mily stood outside the kitchen and dry laundry door.
The yard before her led to the stable and outbuildings
beyond. The sun glowed in the sky as big fluffy clouds
waltzed past on the warm breeze. She chewed a scrap of pitted
apple that she'd grabbed on her way through the kitchen. The
fruit pleasantly soured her mouth.

Not another naughty encounter all morning. Thank
goodness. It was past noontime and she had expected to see
something… What, she hadn't an inkling. The normalcy of the
day was reassuring and proof her mind had run off with the
possibilities.

She inhaled and the smell of sweet rose soap from the
laundry filled her nostrils. If she took stock, the morning was
filled with accomplishment and calm.

She had pulled linens from the beds, washed them, and
now they hung before her, drying on the lines in the floral
summer breeze. She would press them when they dried and
refit others in the rooms of the master, his sons and the ruby

guest room. That was as soon as she found Sibila. Where had she gone? She was uncertain what her next task should be.

She glanced across the white, billowing walls of hanging sheets in the dry laundry and down the rust-colored dirt path, which led to the stone coach house and stalls.

She sighed.

A young man dressed in a green livery long coat and brown breeches crossed the path to the stable with a bucket in hand. His reddish hair curled over his collar. He glanced over his shoulder at her, slowed his pace and fully turned toward her.

Emily froze mid-chew. His green eyes sparkled like a bead of dew caught in the sunlight. Filled with merriment and mirth, he had masculine lips that turned up in a grin and stretched the skin over his square chin.

Her cheeks, filled with apple not yet swallowed, twitched as her lips curved in reply. My, he was handsome. If not for his livery, she'd have taken him for a playful forest sprite. A fiery-haired sprite and an enchanted soul.

He raised his hand and his index finger glided along his lower lip. His tongue slid out and wrapped the tip as long, amber lashes closed over his left eye. He then gestured with his head that she should come with him.

Her heart hammered. He was worth whatever this house was about. She wondered what mischievous, good-natured fun he was headed for. Or did he simply wish her to help with something? She worried her lower lip between her teeth.

He shrugged, turned and continued on his path into the stables, whistling a happy tune.

Sibila stepped out the door past Emily, bringing with her the savory smell of baking apples, cinnamon and tart.

Emily flinched and sucked in a startled breath. Had she been behind her all this time?

"He is handsome, isn't he?" Sibila turned and glanced over her shoulder. "An amazing futter."

A futter... Surely not everyone participated in the act with everyone else here. Or did they?

"Follow me, Emily. Learn something." Sibila's hips gently swayed as she followed the red earth path of sin to the fiery-haired groomsman in the barn.

Emily stared at the barn door as if through a tunnel. *You do want to be introduced to him, so follow her.* Emily glanced back at the door to the kitchen. *Make haste before the cook sees you!*

Emily stepped and her knees wobbled. Her heart pounded. Indeed she wanted to meet him. She inhaled deeply, summoning her fortitude, then gathered up her skirt and ran down the path, across the cobbled drive, to the stable door.

She pressed her back up against the bumpy stone of the barn to the right of the door and closed her eyes, listening.

Crunch, crunch, crunch. Stomp, stomp. Swish, swish. Crunch, crunch.

The horses chewed on their hay and stomped flies away. Her shoulders relaxed. She acted foolishly. *Well, go on in.* It was possible Sibila and the groomsman were...well, she supposed they could be doing anything.

She turned and entered the small barn. Light shined in through the paned windows, casting a golden glow in streams on the dark hall and stalls. The damp air from the cool stone chilled up her skirt like icy fingers. It was as if she entered not into a sprite's den, but something infinitely more sinister.

She inhaled to steady herself and glanced around. Horses resided in the first two stalls. The smell of dry hay and the unique scent of beast and sweat curled into her nostrils. Her muscles tensed. She'd always enjoyed the smell of the barn. It reminded her of long days spent occupying herself while her father readied the horses for the carriage. Though the smells and sounds were similar here, there was a stimulating heated noise to the air which she could not quite place. She strained to hear it more clearly. There was a rustling of cloth and whispered voices.

She stepped forward, carefully listening. She turned the corner and headed down another longer row of stalls with a green door at its end.

"There she is, Adam," Sibila whispered from the stall to the left of Emily. "I told you she would follow."

"Miss Grey." His deep voice, so different from what she'd imagined, made the hairs on her neck stand and her stomach flutter. "Come in and assist us."

Emily peered through the slats in the wood, but saw only hazy light and shadows. What were they about? Maybe they simply required her help with something.

Emily lifted the wooden latch on the stall door and pulled it to the right, sliding it out of the way. She stepped in and quickly closed it behind her.

The copper-haired groomsman faced away from her. His green coat lay fanned out on the hay before him, and he stood in his white shirt and brown breeches. "Umm." A wet, slopping sound came from in front of him.

She stepped closer, and her head spun slightly from the stifling confines of the small space.

"You require my assistance with something…sir?"

"God, yes." His hips pressed forward and then relaxed.

Emily stepped closer. Goodness, he was taller and broader at this vantage than he had appeared from a distance in the dry laundry. His stature was impressive. Definitely not a sprite. She barely came to his shoulders. She rounded his side.

Sibila knelt before him. Her skirts billowed out around her. Hands on his thighs, she licked the length of his peg with an improper slurping sound.

Emily's eyes widened. Oh! She should not be watching this. This was definitely something obscene. The hairs on her neck stood and tingled. They had asked her here to assist them! She could not look away. Long, thick and red, his staff stood straight from his trousers.

"No need to fret, little one. Sibila told me of your innocence and desires. We shall show you nothing more."

Her desires to wed before acting. She relaxed. Thank goodness Sibila had told him. Emily could not take her eyes from Sibila and what she was doing with his prick. Who would have thought? Never. My. Um…

Sibila's red lips glided up his length to the tip and then she sucked the crown into her mouth. She rocked her head forward and back as if she licked a large, spear-shaped sucker. She appeared to enjoy this act, but what did that taste like? It couldn't taste good… Or could it?

"Mmmm." Adam closed his eyes as if he savored a good bit of custard, then reopened them. "See how Sibila does that with her tongue, Miss Grey?" His body shook. "That feels bloody good. Try to remember that when you are asked to do this." He reached out, grasped the green cap on Sibila's head and clenched. "Ummm." His hips pressed forward, and the length of his peg disappeared deep into Sibila's mouth.

Emily's throat tightened, and she swallowed as if he had shoved his peg into her mouth. *When* she was asked to do this?

Could she do this? She wanted to back away, but her feet were cast of stone. *Hold fast, Emily. What harm could it do to watch?* They had asked for her assistance after all. This might help her in the marriage bed. She trembled as her corset rubbed her nipples in a way that it had never done so before. Her chest tightened, and she labored to breathe.

Adam's tall, broad frame shuddered and shook. Emily stared at his round, hard arms and then she glanced lower, down to his waist, his buttocks. His hips rotated forward and his bottom clenched. Amazing that a woman's mouth could cause his well-muscled frame to strain and shudder so. It was as if he worked some impossible task he so desired but struggled to obtain.

"Enough!" He pulled back.

Emily's gaze shot straight to his bright red prick and Sibila's mouth.

Sibila lips flared open. Her tongue lapped out and her eyes closed. His prick slid crimson and glistening from her tongue.

Sibila sat back on her heels, and her sensuous blue eyes fluttered open. "My turn, Adam."

"Indeed it is, but let us involve Miss Grey." He extended his hand to Sibila and helped her to rise to her feet. "Miss Grey." His emerald eyes, a sliver engulfed by passion, captured her.

May lightning strike me still! Emily's eyes widened, and her stomach flipped. The desire in those eyes immobilized her and unwantedly inspired a deep repressed part of her soul. In that exact instant, she wanted him to desperately want her. She glanced at Sibila and then back to him.

His gaze swept her body and settled on her hands in a wave of heat. His eyes shone with that desire. Could he be her one love?

Silliness, Emily, silliness. No other person can enter one's soul with a stare, and he was futtering another. Still—she ripped her gaze to Sibila, hoping for some gesture to bring her back to reality. There was something about Adam.

"What did you have in mind, Adam?" Sibila grinned at Emily and winked.

Winked! As if all this were an acceptable existence. Sibila was scandalous...and wanton...and, well, intriguing. If Emily were to survive and keep her innocence in this house, she needed to know more, and Sibila seemed happy to trust her, show her and be her confidant. Her stomach filled with flutters.

"I would like Miss Grey to place me into your sheath."

Emily closed her eyes. That required her to act. *Fortitude.* She reopened them.

"What a delightful and a wonderful first experience for her." Sibila's blue eyes danced with mischief. "Don't you think, dearest Emily?"

"Ummmm." She would have to touch him and her. Her heart lodged in her throat. The words simply would not form to express the myriad emotions that swirled in her. Fear of losing her innocence and her dreams. Fear of losing her post, and curiosity of what this act entailed with Adam. The contradictions.

She stared at Adam's peg, and her tongue slid out and nervously wet her lips. Heat as warm as the sun outside blazed to her cheeks, and her stomach flipped. No matter how wrong it was, the desire to touch him pulsed through her. She could not admit out loud to her longing, but touching was not the full act. She would still be a virgin when she walked out of the stall. She should embrace this moment and touch him.

"I will take that delightful blush as a confirmation with an exclamation point." Sibila's smile widened further.

"Very good, then." Adam turned to Emily, his prick poking out at her as if it were a sword ready to joust. "Touch me."

Emily's throat tightened and her body tingled as heat bloomed through her gut and pulsed wetly between her legs. She squirmed at the moisture and raised a trembling hand toward him as if reaching for the blade on a sharp knife. "I-I... don't know what to do."

Sibila's fingers glided along the top of Emily's hand, soothing her trembling.

From a dream floating above them, Emily watched Sibila pull her hand to Adam's peg. Her fingers wrapped Emily's about his stiffness. Skin smoother than anything she had touched before met her fingers, and the heat... The feverish temperature warmed her uncommonly cold hand. She cradled his prick in her palm in awe.

"Hold me firmly. The sensation is better when you do."

Emily tightened her grip, and her gaze skipped to Adam's lustful eyes for approval.

"Very good." He nodded. "Sibila, show her how to hand-frig me."

Sibila moved to the other side of Adam. Her hand interlaced overtop of Emily's fingers. "Glide your hand with mine, Emily."

Her hand slid down Adam's peg, and Emily's hand below hers glided along the smooth skin to the bristly hairs at the base.

"Mmm. Yes. Lovely. Leave go, Sibila, and let her do the stroking while you kiss me."

Sibila released her grip on his cock, then grabbed Emily about the hips. She pulled Emily as if she were a doll and placed her so that she stood directly behind Adam, then pressed her body firmly up against his hard, taut back. Emily's arm wrapped his waist as her hand glided repeatedly up and down his staff.

"Excellent thought, Sibila. Fasten your skirts up as she strokes me from behind." Every word and breath vibrated through her torso.

His muscular back against her bosom and his bottom pressing into her stomach made the small stall spin about her. She had never been this close to a man. She leaned her cheek against his back as her hand continued to stroke him. His heart pounded beneath her ear, and she sighed. She floated in the hazy desire and lust that consumed the stall. There was no escape, and her deep, inner longing slowly peeled out of its cage, rushing to her fingers wrapped so firmly about his peg.

"Damn good, little one. Continue to stroke me just so." His entire body jerked.

Emily inhaled to try to steady herself. A musky scent mixed with the smell of straw and beast overwhelmed her. His smell...she inhaled again. He was not the sprite she'd seen in the dry laundry yard, but a feral, mystical creature of sin. She wanted to capture that smell and him. She wanted to make Adam hers.

My goodness, she had never had that inclination upon sighting a man. Her heart pounded, and the flesh between her thighs wept as her eyes should be weeping.

She came here for a post and she just may have found something more rare. Bliss pulsed through her. It did feel good.

Warmth radiated up Adam's back. Emily's hand stroked up to the crown of his cock, and sparks touched his bollocks. He clenched his teeth and breathed deep into his chest. "Sibila, you have such wonderful legs. Position your bottom and legs up on the hay ledge. I am going to fuck you hard and soundly."

Sibila's hips sashayed as she backed away from him. Her eyes lit deviously. She knew what she was about, but Miss Grey? Sibila had asked him to help her learn. Said Miss Grey was innocent and wanted to learn as much as she could as quickly as possible. Was that truth or intrigue? Sibila had lied to him before. Hell, she had fibbed to everyone here at least once.

Miss Grey's hand continued to stroke him as if made for him. Each stroke sent sparks tingling through his sac. He gritted his teeth. Was Sibila sure she was innocent? She certainly acted the part, but that hand-frigging was exquisite. More so. She could bring him to his knees.

What he did know was that the more Miss Grey knew about futtering, the more this house would only work to her advantage. Having him protect her was even more important, as everyone here had their secrets.

He had yet to figure which of the sons Sibila was so dearly attached to. She was wicked enough to make things her way, no matter how tough and cunning the opponent. He had no reason to get in her way with Miss Grey. Unless her amore involved Devlin.

Besides, Miss Grey was far prettier than Sibila had let on. She was small, with an oval face and rich brown hair that caught fire from the sun. Her pale complexion made her appear frail. Combine that with her obscure, dancing hazel eyes and Miss Grey reached deep to Adam's protective streak.

He figured Sibila had initiated this teaching because the new girl threatened her in some way, though Adam didn't know what that might be. At first he'd thought only to have fun with the two girls, but now he'd met Miss Grey, he wanted to look out for her and help her find her way here. Right now, it seemed the best way to do so was to participate in whatever Sibila asked.

Miss Grey's petite hands stroked his hard cock. She reached the ridge at the crown and squeezed. Small, heated bursts of erotic delight erupted in him like sappy wood placed on the fire. Sweat dampened his brow, and he sucked in a breath. Wicked. Delightful. Delicate yet firm, her hands were unlike any other girl's he had experienced. He glanced down at his purplish red cock, and the size of her fingers made him appear bigger than he was. What man wouldn't like that view?

"I am going to step forward, Miss Grey. Keep stroking me and simply move with me when I do." He stepped forward.

She moved with him. Her hands continued to frig him and not one moment did her body lose contact with his back.

His chest constricted. There was something so endearing in her movements. She clung to him, pleasuring him, yet trembled erotically simply from pressing to him. It was as if she was adrift in the erotic sea created by being near him.

Only a handful of sentences had left her mouth since she'd stepped into the stall, not enough to know her by, but her voice was delightful. He would bet his month's pay there was an intelligent mind in her head. After this futter, he would find out.

He reached Sibila. She slid her hands about his shoulders, and her lips touched his. Softly she traced her tongue along his lower lip, and then sucked the pout between her teeth. A moan escaped his chest. God, that felt good. The combination of Sibila teasing his mouth and Miss Grey fondling his cock was enough to have him spending in five strokes. *No! You need to show restraint. Show Miss Grey how this should be done.*

He reached out and ran his fingers along the soft flesh just above Sibila's stockings on the inside of her thighs.

"Oh yes, Adam. Touch me. Pinch me," Sibila mumbled into his mouth.

He grabbed command of her lips and pressed back, thrusting his tongue deep between her teeth and along her tongue. She tasted of coffee. His brow pulled tight. *Never mind that. Fuck her.*

He slid his fingers up her thigh and pinched her inner thigh hard. Sibila squirmed against him, lightly crying out into their kiss. He released the flesh and continued to trail his fingers higher up the slope of her leg and into Sibila's creamy cunt lips.

She was good and wet and delightfully fragrant too. There would be no problem diddling her as hard as he wanted to. He rocked his hips forward in a fucking motion. The front of his waist pressed against Sibila's open thighs. His finger dipped into her hole and she bucked, sliding his fingers farther into her wet cunt. He moaned. She moaned. His prick wept desire from its tip. Miss Grey's hand slickened, gliding along his stiffness with increased ease. She moaned ever so faintly.

Miss Grey's hips swayed forward and back, locked to him. Her mound rubbed against his bum and thighs. She was just as aroused as Sibila, yet he could not see her longing expression. "Reach around with your other hand, Miss Grey, and touch Sibila."

Miss Grey's muscles tensed about him, her hand gripping his cock harder. Delightful. More wetness leaked from his tip. He groaned. He didn't want to push her, but much more would happen to her in this house. She needed to know, and wanted to learn quickly, so this was the best way.

Sibila reached around his shoulder and touched Miss

Grey's hair in a loving caress. Miss Grey's muscles liquefied. Her hand trailed his waist to his stomach. He slid his fingers out of Sibila and reached for Miss Grey's hand.

His wet fingers entwined with her trembling ones and he pulled her hand to Sibila's cunny. "A single touch, Miss Grey, as I want you to know what my cock will experience as you place me inside her."

He put her hand on Sibila's mound and released it. She needed to enter her on her own. He would not force her.

Sibila moaned and arched her hips toward him and Miss Grey's hand. "Oh! Oh. Yes, Emily. Slide all the way in." She reached over his shoulder and gripped Miss Grey's hair.

Miss Grey's fingers disappeared inside of Sibila. Adam's heart jumped into his throat, and his sack tightened. She did it. "Is your cunt as wet, Miss Grey?"

Miss Grey pulled her hand back, still trembling. Her body shook against him. "Y-yes." Her voice came out a whisper.

"Good little girl. Grasp my cock again."

Her fingertips trailed along his length and, one by one, each oiled finger gripped him.

Lightning shot up his spine. He quaked and recaptured Sibila's mouth, desperately wishing he kissed Miss Grey. His tongue twined with Sibila's, and she pulled back. She reached beneath his arms and back to Miss Grey. Her arms trailed up and down.

What was she doing? He glanced down. She caressed Miss Grey. Her hands stroked her sides and her breasts. He leaned forward and placed a wet kiss on Sibila's ear. "Can you reach her nipples, wicked girl?"

She nodded against his head and then kissed his cheek. Her arms brushed up his sides.

"When I flex my hips forward, Miss Grey, I wish you to glide my cock all the way into Sibila." He waited.

He wanted Miss Grey's nipples to be pinched by Sibila as he entered her. He listened for the quick intake of breath behind him and flexed his hips. Her hands glided him forward, and the tip of him touched hot velvet oil. He pushed farther forward, and her fingers unwrapped as he slid all the way in.

Sibila cried out and her arms jerked as the spongy walls of her cunt clamped onto him.

Miss Grey groaned behind him and arched her hips against his bottom, searching for a release she would be denied in this moment, but not for long. Miss Grey's hand slid up his belly, trapped between him and Sibila.

He pulled back to allow her to free her hand, but she did not move. Her fingers fluttered there, touching his wet cock and Sibila's hairs between them. He pushed forward. Her hips moved with him. She danced with him in primal need.

Sibila's hands trembled, rubbing up and down his sides. Miss Grey's mound ground against his bottom as his cock stroked in and out of Sibila's greedy cunt. Her flesh pulled at his thickness, caressing every inch of his prick.

His sac tightened and tingles shot down to the soles of his feet. He gritted his teeth. He needed to hold back, to last longer. The urge to fuck harder and harsher washed through him, and the will to prolong this lust unwound like a thread.

Miss Grey's rocking hips controlled him.

He wanted her to come. To see her unravel as her soft voice screamed out in ecstasy.

No, Adam! Don't think about that.

It is too late. Damn it!

He pushed forward hard, banging Sibila back against the stall wall. "Ugh."

Don't spill. Don't!

Sibila cried out. This was the kind of fucking she craved from him. He knew that. Hard and driving. It was what he craved too. He couldn't hold back. Her cunt clasped tightly to him in coils of wanton hunger.

His entire body tensed. He exploded, bucking hard and fast into her as the wall rattled behind her. Light flashed before him, and he spilled, his sac pulsing in a release he could not stop.

He stilled, panting, and closed his eyes as everything about him hummed. Damn, that was powerful.

Sibila leaned back. "I do believe, Adam, that is the first time you have spent before me. Do I take credit for your overwhelming lust or should I give that credit to Miss Grey?"

Adam swallowed again. Damn it. He couldn't bloody well tell her it was Miss Grey's swaying hips and tingling hands. That would only vex her entirely.

Miss Grey loosened her hold about his waist.

Adam stepped back as did Miss Grey, and Sibila dropped her legs to the ground before him. "Well, Adam?"

"Having the two of you was my undoing." That was true.

She frowned at him and narrowed her rapidly cooling eyes. "We have sheets to fit, Emily." Sibila ran her hands down her skirts. "Are you ready?"

Miss Grey nodded to Sibila, but said nothing.

Sibila walked past Adam and Miss Grey and pulled the door open. She stepped out of the stall and disappeared up the aisle. Miss Grey turned to follow.

"Wait, Miss Grey." Adam stepped toward her. Her cheeks held a delightful flush of passion and her cap had been tipped askew from holding tight to him as he thrashed into Sibila. A smile curved his lips. Adorable. The only thing missing was kiss-swollen lips.

He reached up and straightened the cap in her thick, wavy hair.

"Thank—"

He leaned down and pressed his closed lips firmly to hers. She sucked in a startled breath, parting her lips to him, and tensed. His tongue swept into her warmth just once. "Mmmmm." She tasted sweet. He pulled back and whispered so low that only she could hear. "You are delightful, Miss Grey. I want to make you shatter in ecstasy. To ease that ache between your legs. Will you permit me to come to you tonight and frig you with my hands?"

He pulled back and stared down into dark greenish blue eyes. She nodded. "All right."

CHAPTER 3

*E*mily lifted her skirts and ran to catch up with Sibila. My goodness. What had she just agreed to? Her head spun and her heart beat wildly. His kiss had been so tender after all that scandalous behaviour. She could not say no. He had tempted her base desires into wanting him to touch her. To do the things he did to Sibila in the barn. Simply sighting him had turned her sensibilities on their sides.

She exited the stables into the dry laundry and spun about. No one was present. Her lips still tingled from the pressure. She raised her hand and touched her lips, as if doing so would preserve the romantic, tender gesture.

She had only been kissed once before by the chipper's son out by the barn when she was sixteen, three years past, and it did none of the things that Adam's kiss had just now.

Her feet moved quickly past the billowing sheets to the green kitchen door. A mix of thyme and sage filtered through the air. She inhaled deeply to steady herself and stepped into the small golden space in search of Sibila.

Miss Wicking, the cook, stood with her back to the three

arched fireplaces. Her hands worked busily, chopping a long ivory-and-green leek on the large cook's table.

"Pray, Miss Wicking, have you seen Sibila? I have lost her."

Miss Wicking looked up, her round face flushed from working by the hot fires. "She passed through here with a stack of linens, Miss Grey. I imagine she can be found on the second floor making beds. Or in one." She rolled her eyes, and the ruddy skin on her plump cheeks crinkled as she chuckled a laugh that sneered.

Emily's brows pinched. Did she not like Sibila?

"Care for a piece of cheese to get you through to dinner, dear? Nan brought a nice bit from the dairy, aged with sage and garlic. 'Tis delightfully saucy with a glass of wine." Miss Wicking picked up a platter in one hand and a glass in the other. "Take a piece and a swallow, then get on your way to finish your tasks. The men shall be back from the day soon, and you house girls will need a little more fortitude."

Emily blew out a tense breath and her stomach sank. The men had been absent all day. Was her afternoon calm simply because the house was empty? Oh dear. If what Sibila said was true, they would request she do things for them as Adam had with Sibila in the barn. Adam. He was worth her figuring out a way to stay here. She needed a plan, some way to keep her dream intact, all while working in this house of sin. She needed all the nerve she could get to fend for herself in this place.

The corner of Miss Wicking's mouth quirked up, and she winked.

Emily frowned and stared at Miss Wicking. She was cheery enough, all alone here in the kitchen, cooking away, seemingly without a fret in the world.

She could use a bit of wine to calm her beating heart. Emily reached out and grasped a piece of soft white cheese with green flecks in it. "Thank you, Miss Wicking." She put a bit of the cheese to her mouth, than grasped the cup of wine, raised it to her lips and swallowed a good mouthful.

The strong fruit flavor mixed with the creamy cheese soothed all the way down her gullet. "Mmmm." That should ease her nerves and restore her wit. Well, maybe just one more sip. She raised the glass and swallowed once more.

"Suggestive, isn't it? Wine and cheese…there is nothing more provocative, not even a futter." Miss Wicking smiled a smile so bright it sparked levity in her green eyes. "That should keep you in good spirits for the rest of the afternoon. Get on now. Finish your chores so that dinner and the engagement festivities won't be spoilt."

Emily smiled at Miss Wicking. An engagement…that could only mean there was some form of morals breathed into this house. "Engagement festivities?"

"Yes, the master hopes to announce the eldest son Mr. Christon's betrothal this weekend. He is speculating it shall be this night. Now shoo."

Emily nodded, hopeful her mind once again was making things concerning the Earl of Gregor worse than the truth. They had to be. For who would be debauched enough to allow everyone in his household to morally commit suicide in the eyes of society? The Earl of Gregor would have to be a warlock himself to allow that kind of shame to befall him, in truth.

She turned and rushed into the main servant's hall. Three paces down, she turned up the stairs to the second set of landings. Slowly, she opened the door onto the hall. She stepped into the corridor which led down to the master's sons' rooms. A dry warmth radiated about her.

This hall was her favorite part of the house so far. Elaborate blue and green tapestry lined the arched walls from mid-molding to the ceiling on the left side. The side to her right was a series of windows from floor to ceiling. The sunlight cut through the windows and warmed the entire space. It was extraordinary.

She stopped and stared out at the view of the back lawn and the grounds to the forest edge. A man stood on the lawn, staring off into the distance as if awaiting some long-lost love. In his high-buttoned, blue-and-grey striped coat and grey trousers, he appeared a fashion plate she had seen on occasion while in town. His black hair glistened in the late afternoon sun. He turned his head and glanced up at the windows, then nodded at her with pursed lips.

Goodness, what was she doing? She had work to do and here she dallied as if leisure was the way of her day. She turned and stepped into the first room on the left in search of Sibila.

She glanced around the crimson room. The clean white satin sheets were fitted and the windows were closed, but no Sibila. Emily stepped back into the hall and walked down to the next bedchamber. Gold tapestry hung on the walls, and a rich dark brown curtain covered the windows. Here too the bed was fitted with new crisp linens.

Had she dallied so long in the kitchen and barn that all the chores had been done without her? She would have some explaining to do when she found Sibila. All her afternoon work had been accomplished. She walked back out into the hall and continued down to the last room on this wing. She turned into the doorway.

Sibila lay on the freshly fitted bed face down, her back gyrating and heaving. Emily sighed. Sibila was entirely single-minded. Her behavior was inhuman, as if she were some animal in heat who could not rest until she achieved futter.

Emily moved slowly into the room. They had work to do. The green sheers billowed out from the open windows, adding fresh midday air to the room. Her pink boots made not a sound on the thick green-and-blue patterned carpet. She leaned down on the bed and touched Sibila's back. "Sibila?"

Sibila stilled and then turned her face toward Emily. Her cheeks flushed. "I am having such an impossible time spending with my hands. I ache for release from Adam's selfishness. Help me, Emily, please." She rolled onto her side. Her brown skirts and petticoat, pulled up to her waist, exposed the soft flannel of her drawers. Her slit lay open, and her fingers rocked back and forth through her dense mass of shining curls. "Please." Desperation filled her blue eyes.

The hairs on the back of Emily's neck stood on end.

Sibila closed her eyes, and an exasperated sigh pressed past her lips. She rolled completely onto her back and spread her knees wide. The fingers of her free hand slid across her belly and pushed the lowest button on the front of her shirt through the hole. Then she moved upward, unbuttoning each of the five buttons that ran down the front.

She pulled the fabric aside, exposing her short corset and chemise of longcloth. Her breasts and nipples formed round swells above the tightened cotton stays.

"I can achieve the relief I desire quickly if you will rub my breasts and pinch my nipples while I frig myself. Will you do this for me, Emily?"

Touch her breasts... Emily stared at her nipples poking up through the fabric. Sibila trembled, and the flesh of her bosom rippled just as Emily envisioned the palpitating orbs in the stories she sometimes read. Indeed. Simply touch her breasts.

That didn't seem too hard. Sibila had, after all, done the exact same thing to her in the barn *You can manage that, Emily. This should not be difficult.* Emily nodded, but her stomach flipped in unease. Once again she found herself in new territory.

"Touch them as I did yours in the barn behind Adam. If you do so, I shall gloriously spend."

The remembered sensation of Adam pressed to her front so tightly assaulted her senses. The smell of his lust lingered in her nostrils, and the flesh between her thighs throbbed.

Sibila squirmed before her, yearning for a release neither of them had achieved on the encounter in the barn.

Adam's words crept back to her conscience: *I want to make you shatter in ecstasy. To ease that ache between your legs. Will you permit me to come to you tonight and frig you with my hands?* Her chest tightened, and the tender kiss he so shockingly pushed upon her tingled her lips anew. Why did thoughts of Adam touching her as Sibila touched herself now wet her thighs so?

Sibila's hand dipped farther into her private place. "Now. Now."

Emily gazed down on Sibila, her eyes closed and her lips slightly parted. She couldn't move and was not certain she wanted to. Logic said she could do so, but her gut, her gut said this was not proper.

"What do we have here?" A deep, male voice rang from the doorway.

Emily jumped and turned her head away from the door as heat blazed to her face. She couldn't look to see who had just entered the room. How humiliating! Her stomach churned sickeningly. She wanted to pull the sheets over herself or crawl beneath the bed. Her entire body stiffened as if she was a man caught in Medusa's gaze. She could not move.

Sibila slid her hand away from her slit and pushed up onto

her elbows. She glanced at Emily and mouthed, *"All is well,"* then stared back toward the door. "Sir, we just finished fitting your bed and—"

"And decided to soil the sheets for me?" His scratchy voice sounded appalled.

This was his room. He was one of the master's sons. Emily slowly slid off the bed, still facing away from him. She bowed her head and turned toward him. Her first day on the job and she had annoyed her employer.

He stepped forward.

Emily glanced up. The same dark-haired young man she'd seen from the window out on the lawn stood before her.

He stopped at the edge of the bed. Impeccably dressed in grey and blue, he stood tall and stiff.

She fisted her hands and rubbed her fingertips against her palms nervously.

With his hands clasped behind his back, his brown eyes stared down at Sibila's red, open cunt.

Emily's eyes widened. She had touched that spot on her, yet she had not known it was so red and puffy.

Reaching out, he touched Sibila's knee. Sibila's tongue darted out and wet her lips.

Emily's heart pounded.

His hand slid down her thigh like a snake heading for its den. He slid his fingers deep inside Sibila. She cried out, arched her hips and tossed her head back.

His smoldering brown eyes turned to Emily and held her stare. "Leave us," his voice graveled.

She flinched. "Yes sir." Emily bobbed a curtsy, turned and picked up the pile of satin linens from the side table.

"Kneel up and place your hands behind your neck," he scolded.

Emily hurried from the room.

What would happen to Sibila? Would he punish her for her rudeness in pleasuring herself on his bed? Outside the door, she paused and tilted her head to try and make out any of their sounds. Nothing. She closed her eyes and shook her head. *Your thoughts are truly monstrous, Emily.* She swallowed hard. This was where *she* was posted. She sighed.

She continued down the hall toward the stairs and the corridor to the other bedchambers. As she passed the brown and gold room, Adam stepped out into the hall from the stairwell.

Emily stopped and tilted her head to the side. What was a groomsman doing in the main house on the sleeping level? "What are you doing here, Adam?" He belonged in the stables...did he not?

"I decided I couldn't wait to hear you scream, Miss Grey. You hardly said three sentences in the barn. I want to hear that lovely voice of yours moan."

The flesh of her thighs tingled simply at his words. "Oh, umm." She swallowed hard. "So you said in the barn." She licked her lips and glanced down at the bundle of linens in her hands, trying to think of any way to postpone this encounter. Her hands trembled. Did she truly want to postpone the encounter? Adam was handsome and, oh, the way he looked at her made her stomach flutter, but she had chores. Dallying instead of doing her work would only cause trouble. "Now is not good. I have to finish fitting sheets."

In two steps, he was in front of her, staring down.

She stepped back. The smell of his body enfolded her, and her knees weakened. She licked her lips.

He reached out. One hand wrapped her waist and the other braced her neck. She stared up into brilliant jade eyes as he pulled her hard up against his front. Her breath locked in the cage of her ribs.

Adam's lips came down on hers and he backed her toward the glass window. She squirmed against him, unsure what to expect, but loving the feel of his firm lips on hers. His tongue darted into her mouth with a hunger like the one he'd stirred within her in the barn. Her breath labored and her heart leapt. She wanted him and this.

This time she wanted to kiss him back. She pushed her tongue against his, wrapping it about the thickness and tasting his spicy essence. He locked his lips to hers and pressed his teeth to her tongue, stilling her movements, then sucked all of her restraint into his being. He stole her breath. Her knees shook and she leaned heavily against him. How was it possible one man made her feel so decadent?

She inhaled, and his scent overwhelmed her. *God, he even smells scandalous.* Clean soap and lustful beast of sin. She wanted to cuddle up with him and bury her nose in all those delicious-smelling crevices.

He released her tongue, and his hands molded her bottom. He pulled her tighter to his front. The bulging hardness of his cock ground against the flesh of her stomach. Her head spun as she remembered his hot skin in her hands. She ran her tongue wantonly along his smooth teeth, wanting to experience every texture he could offer.

He pulled back from her lips. Intense lust-filled green eyes stared into hers. "You are bewitching, Miss Grey." He swallowed, and the bump in his throat bobbed.

His hands about her waist rotated her so that she faced the large glass pane. "Take your hands, Miss Grey, and put your palms flat on the glass."

"All right." Her voice came out hoarse and breathy.

Goodness… He even made her sound a wanton. She pressed her hands to the warmed surface and gazed out at the empty lawn.

He leaned down and grasped the material of her skirt and petticoat. Her heart jumped into her throat as the soft fabric trailed up her legs and he tucked the loose material into the band of her skirts.

She now stood uncovered from the waist down, her drawers, stockings and pink boots exposed for anyone to see. She trembled. He would touch her the same way he had touched Sibila in the barn. She swallowed hard. Being exposed for him, for anyone to see, sent excited heat between her thighs and scared her. Could she do this here, now, with him? She glanced nervously over her shoulder at him and licked her lips. His red hair curled in short wisps about his face and the look of desire in his eyes shot tickles down her belly. Save her, she wanted him. She let out a jagged breath.

A deep chuckle erupted from his chest. "Nervous?"

She nodded, unable to find her voice.

"I won't go farther than you have already given me permission, Miss Grey."

His hands…he would only use his hands.

He pressed himself fully to her. His hands rubbed up her sides and along her arms, making her body ripple in their wake. His fingers intertwined with hers on the glass and squeezed. His warm lips softly kissed the side of her cheek. She tilted her head toward him, and a small moan caught in her throat. These sensations were passion. What he stirred in her was lust. Yet his soft kisses said so much more to her. His kisses contented her.

His tongue trailed to her ear. Warm and wet, it swirled into the cup. Tingles raised all the hairs on her neck and shot down her spine.

Her body jerked, arching back against him as if it were a piece of wood being strung into an archer's bow. He released her fingers and stepped to the side.

Touches trailed pleasure down her side to the swell of her bottom. He played with the loose cotton fabric of the slit of her drawers.

Her breath jittered out. She wanted him to touch her bare flesh.

His hand glided onto her bottom and stilled. Heat seeped into her bare skin.

Crests of sensation surged up her back, and she sucked in a breath. The muscles of her bottom clenched. Oh. Oh. That was better than she had imagined.

His lips brushed against her ear. "I want you to use your voice, Miss Grey. You have such a seductive tone."

Seductive? Never had anyone said that about her voice before. "All right." Her voice came out a choked whisper. She squeezed her eyes closed. That was far from an alluring tone.

"It appears you need more instruction. When something feels good and you want to moan, cry out, purr like a cat or whatever, do so with big tone."

She could do that. But what if someone heard?

"Miss Grey?"

"Adam."

His hand moved on her bottom, caressing her dewed skin in tiny circles, heading toward her crack. With each loop his fingers made, her muscles pulsed with prickling heat.

His fingers delved into the crack of her bottom and dove down, grazing her pucker and into the flesh of her cunny.

She jerked, then held perfectly still. Her eyes opened unseeing on the world below her.

His hand cupped her humid flesh, not entering her or parting her as the doctor had so quickly done. The tips of his fingers touched her curls, and his palm covered her entire slit. He held his hand there, unmoving.

She trembled and bit her lip. She wanted to wiggle her hips to rub against his hand and show him her need.

His tongue glided along the curve of her ear, and she sighed in a hazy bliss.

"Tone," he whispered firmly into her ear.

She moaned deep.

"Better." He pressed his frame against her back, pressing her breasts against the glass. The radiance from the sun warmed her skin as if she were a cat lounging in the hallway. "*Purrr…!*"

His lips curved against her ear. "Excellent."

Thank goodness. If it had not been, her cheeks would be the color of an apple instead of simply pink.

His tongue lapped the lobe of her ear and his lips closed over the drop of flesh, pulling it into his mouth.

"Ummm." Tingles raced her skin.

He chuckled deep in his chest. Then he released her flesh.

All she could do was experience this man pressed against her. Her body reacted in beautiful ways she could not control. She wanted more.

Adam's hand rocked gently back and forth. Folding his hand like a cup, he pinched her nether lips together, then increased both the pressure and the force of his back-and-forth motion.

Emily squirmed and slid her feet farther apart on the floor. Oh how she wanted him to enter her body. To put one of his fingers in her as the doctor had. She pushed her bottom back against him. "Please." The word came out a whisper.

"Miss Grey." His tone scolded.

Oh God, he wanted her to say it louder. To admit for anyone to hear how wanton she was. She shifted and pushed her feet apart, hoping he would simply understand.

"You need to ask with tone, Miss Grey." He continued to jostle her back and forth. Her flesh grew wetter and wetter. The sounds of his hand suctioning against her drenched skin reached her ears. The sounds... Her body jerked and her breath labored. She moaned loudly.

"Good, little one. Ask."

His teeth grazed her neck and bit. She squirmed. Her blood pulsed forcefully beneath his teeth. He did not let go, but continued to apply pressure. His hand rocked her hips and body, slipping back and forth.

Tingles pulsed through her womb, and her knees weakened, threatening to send them both to the floor. Little pops of light flashed to her eyes. A deep, primal need to have him join with her vibrated her soul. She wanted more than his fingers parting her folds. Fever swept her body. The feel of his wet peg joining his and Sibila's body in intimate bliss bounced around unwanted in her mind. She wanted him to be the one. Her heart would belong to him. She trembled uncontrollably.

He released the bite and blew a long stream of humid breath against the spot. Her body jerked. She needed release. She didn't care who heard. "Please! Please! Adam, make me—"

His middle finger pushed down through her slick lips and parted her.

Her eyes widened as her flesh bloomed open. "Oh!" Her

inner muscles contracted and sucked his finger deep within her slit. "Oh!" A warm wave of pressure erupted in her gut.

He moved his hand and slid the tip of another finger to the opening of her hole. Pushing up, he stretched her lips wide and slid both fingers all the way into her sheath.

A small pain caressed her flesh, and she bit her lip.

His other hand wrapped about her waist to the place the pressure grew and grew. He spread his palm over the flesh below her corset, above the top of her mound. He pressed inward. His fingers slid in and out repeatedly.

The sounds of him finger-frigging her lapped along her nerves with each heightened sensation.

Her legs spread farther apart. She squirmed. She needed more. More of the pleasure of him.

"Let go, let the pleasure take you."

She erupted. Her cunny clasped in waves to his fingers as her body convulsed, banging against the glass and against him. "Oh! Oh! Delightful!" She had never... Oh... Who knew?

The spasms of her muscles slowed, and she leaned her heated cheek against the glass and blinked. Slowly, focus returned. She glanced out at the lawn.

Below her, three men stood, staring up and watching her. She gasped and squeezed her eyes shut before she could take in their details. She did not want to know who witnessed her wanton unraveling. Gracious, what had she just done?

"Not horrid, was it, Miss Grey?" He slowly pulled his hand from between her thighs. She swallowed, leaning heavily against the glass. He slid his forearms beneath her arms and pulled her up so that her legs were straight. Not that she was certain she could support herself.

Emily glanced down at his hands wrapped about her

breasts. The one that had been inside her was covered in slick, glossy moisture and a tinge of blood.

She closed her eyes. Had he taken her virginity with his hands? Was that possible? No, not truly. Either way, she was no longer innocent in the true sense of the word. He had broken her restraint. Tempted her. She had hoped to wait until she was wed.

Guilt sliced down her spine, pressing deep into her gut, and churned acidic. Her dreams of love, marriage and family teetered on what he would do. What she would do. Where they would go from here. What if he didn't like her the way she liked him? He could simply be a dog with his nose on the table of life and she was one more morsel. The way he gazed at her said so much more. Still, she was uncertain. Tears welled in her eyes, and her throat tightened.

She turned toward Adam, needing to be held, and buried her face into his shoulder. Her chest heaved and the tears trickled slowly.

He wrapped his arms tightly about her and gently rubbed her shoulder blades. Such a caring gesture. He did care. Her lip wobbled, and she could not hold back the tide of tears that took her.

CHAPTER 4

*B*aited, and he bit. Sibila made a cake of him.

Adam pulled Miss Grey tighter to him. Her chest heaved as if she had no room for anything but tears. Allowing her body to release the emotions this day had pressed upon her was the only thing he could do. He had learned that sometimes a woman simply needed to let tide of emotions out, then things would settle and be fine.

He was, in many senses, relieved it was him to have her tears rather than one of the masters, the doctor, or Sibila.

Sibila had deceived him. He should have talked to Miss Grey more before…well, before introducing her further to the house's ways. He should have known better than to let his desire invade his thoughts.

Miss Grey was not eager to learn of futter. No woman would cry as such if she had been.

His teeth clenched tightly. This was beyond anything he had thought Sibila capable of. Being of easy virtue was one sin, but this…this proved she cared for no one. Not one whit. Who was he kidding?

No one here did.

They all would use this pure, intimate gesture Miss Grey had bestowed on him to tangle her and bend her to their needs. He could not allow that. His stomach churned with unease.

Her body stilled against his chest, and she sniffled. He gently rubbed her back, waiting for her to pull up and away from him as he had seen his mother do after a fit of tears.

"I am sorry, Adam." Her voice, a muffled sound mixed in humid puffs, licked against his neck.

His neck twitched and arched, wanting that moist caress from her mouth to slide up as the echo of her release still clamored in his ears. His lips curled up against her hair. What a quandary. Here she needed to apologize, and he only wanted her more. A scoundrel, he was, for not speaking to her first. No better than the likes of them. He gritted his teeth. "There is no need to fret, Miss Grey. This day, I am certain, has been something of an emotional storm." It was proving to be so, even for him.

She sniffled again, her hands fisting against his waistband along his sides. "I simply had no idea this is what I would be doing when I arrived. My parents both worked here years ago, and being their daughter secured me this position with Mr. Waterton."

Ah. A tremor raced from her hands resting on his hips down through Adam's bottom. He forced his gaze out at the lawn and away from the subtle movements of her soft body so he could concentrate on her words. The man who had changed this house forever stood in the clearing, staring out at the pond. Her mum had no idea!

The new Lord Gregor was a scoundrel of extreme vulgarity.

By the time her mother knew of the changes, it would be far too late for her to save her daughter's soul.

She sighed, and her chest rubbed against his. He closed his eyes, unable to concentrate on anything but the woman in his arms. Soft, feminine innocence.

Sort this out, Adam.

He inhaled a breath that held no comfort. The scent of roses brought a hazy longing for days slowly bedding this woman as she screamed in pleasure again and again. *Not what you should be thinking about.* Had he fallen so far down the debauched path?

She swallowed hard against his shoulder. Lord Gregor would have her, and so would his sons.

In many, many unsavory ways.

A chill raised all the hairs on his neck. Damn. He needed to know more about why she remained here after learning what this house was. No woman who cried in his arms deserved what Portage Place brought forth. Especially seeing as she had held on to her virginity. She couldn't want this.

"Your mum is in service, then?" Adam's throat tightened in dread of what the masters would expose Miss Grey to.

"Was. At Chesterfield Hall. The home of the Marquess of Brenton before he closed it up." Her cheek rubbed against his shoulder in a gesture that shone warmth and need on him as if the sun warmed his skin on a rainy day.

His muscles relaxed into her. This was the most intimate gesture he had experienced in this house in the two years of his service. Surprising. He had not realized until this instant that he missed simply being needed…needed in the most simple of ways, to be held and to hold someone in more than release. His throat closed on his breath. He tightened his muscles around her and swallowed the lump lodged in his throat. "Was?"

"Yes, she and my father have both passed on six months past. A carriage accident."

She was alone. "Do you have any other relatives, Miss Grey?"

"No."

Gently laying the side of his face against the soft cap atop of her head, he inhaled a broken breath—someone needed to protect her—and moved his hand around her shoulder. The scent of her arousal still clung to his fingers and mixed with her tears now staining the cloth of his livery. His heart clamored, willing him to soothe her, to take her and make all her fears go away. To be the man of morals he used to be.

Impossible. You are here for Devlin, no one else. You cannot save her and be what you must here. No matter that it would be best if she left. You need to remove her, for your sanity and her own good. Do what you must. He gathered his wits and blew out an exaggerated breath.

"Miss Grey, there is nothing in nature wrong with anything you have done or seen here. Even though society has made the act into what they call *sin*." Her muscles stiffened against him as if the word alone caused her fits. His fingers gently rubbed her back and shoulder. His will soothed her, when he could not let his words. "Sin bothers you, Miss Grey. Well, sin is what this house thrives on."

Her chest stopped moving against his, creating a physical barrier of air between them.

He pressed on, determined to make his point. "Have you ever had longing, Miss Grey? Sinful things you have desired with a man?"

She carefully nodded against his shoulder.

"We all have those longings, and here in this house every longing you have or someone else has about you is permitted without their or your permission. Tell me, Miss Grey, what is it you long for with a man?" It was not to be standing here in this hell with him, for that he was certain.

They stood motionless for five ticks of the clock as he waited for her reply.

She softly cleared her throat. "I want to marry..." Her fingers gripped the fabric of his coat. "...a man I love, and to explore those sinful longings with him," she said with conviction.

All the hairs on his arms stood. Foolishness. He held in a laugh, but his chest heaved against the strain. She wanted lust *and* marriage? He had thought that possible once. But then...

His father had left his mother.

His mother had slept with Lord Gregor.

Lady Gregor had taken a lover and run off.

Marriage and passion were oil and water. They pooled around each other, but never made anything that caused cravings.

Besides, someone always hurt or left the other, following a lust that was not for whom they wed. A lust that was not for whom they loved.

"That is a nice fancy, Miss Grey, but not one based in reality. Especially in *your* position here."

She swallowed hard against him...twice.

His words were hard to swallow, indeed. The truth sometimes was. "A dream I am sure that is difficult to give up." Maybe her parents had been passionately happy together, but if they were, they were a sideshow oddity. She had to realize that. Life in their station had no room for love.

"A dream I won't dismiss, Adam," she whispered and

sniffled again, rubbing the side of her face against his brown coat. "I am here. I know what is required of me. That does not define who I am."

"No. Indeed, it does not." His suspicion was confirmed. She did not belong here. "Love and marriage *may* be possible, Miss Grey, but lust and marriage I have *never* seen. Lust is what this house thrives on. Please consider what I said. And if you want your dream, leave here now." He held in a cringe as his voice rang harshly even to his own ears. He fisted his fingers in the fabric of her skirt, wanting her to stay next to him even as he told her to leave.

He didn't want to see her nature crushed. Why he cared so much for her happiness when they'd just met, he didn't know. But he did, and his gut had never been wrong yet.

She pushed up and away from him. Her jaw set and her eyes glimmered with tears. "I am not ready to leave here."

He fought with the muscles of his arms not to shake her. "Oh, yes you are, and will, Miss Grey. With certainty I can tell you in this house the men will want nothing more than to take pleasure from you. They will not wait for your permission. They will not offer you love or marriage. They will offer lust, forced lust. Nothing more." They were harsh words she needed to hear. He would protect her as much as he could. He could not let her stand alone here, but if the master or his sons asked for her, she would have no choice but to do what they asked or lose her position, and he could not stop them. Or could he? No, not without jeopardizing his last words to his mother. He promised he would watch over Devlin, his half-brother. He could not put that in jeopardy.

"Sibila said she would show me what I needed to know to survive here." She pulled back farther and stared at him with hardening green eyes. "And all you can tell me is to leave?"

Her jaw set higher, and her lip wobbled. "Sibila will help me find my way through all of this." She pulled her arms back, trying to free herself. His hands tightened on her.

Damn Sibila for getting inside her mind. Sibila would ruin her at her first opportunity to get what she wanted. "You would learn more about the trials of life and untamed lust from that slag, that is for certain, Miss Grey, but you won't obtain the dreams you mentioned." He glanced again out at the lawn and the master. Dread bubbled hot and poisonous through his gut as protection and anger fought to gain possession of him. *Relax, Adam. She will eventually understand. She cannot be your concern.* He fisted his hands. "If you stay, this house will, without fail, eat your heart for supper."

Miss Grey tilted her head to the side, her chocolate-colored brows pulled tight as she frowned. "Adam, I—"

"Shhh. There is no need to say more. You simply don't belong here. Leave." This was the correct thing for him to do.

"I have no other post, Adam." Miss Grey shook her head. "I have other dreams that don't involve men. Dreams of survival. Dreams of being in service. How dare you assume to know me by asking one question." She turned from him, wrenching her arms from his grasp, and picked up her linens. "I have chores to finish."

"Miss Grey."

She paused and glanced back at him. Her eyes questioned him from beneath her long, mink lashes. In the sunlight, her tears dried in streaks down her flushed face. His chest tightened.

He reached up and trailed his fingers into the hair on the back of her head, turning her toward him. His thumb glided along her tightening, damp cheek. "I wish I could do more for you, Miss Grey." Damn, she was so irresistible. *She will be torn apart here.*

He leaned in and pressed his lips to her plush, frowning ones in a breath of longing for more of her innocence, and regret that he would never have her himself. Couldn't. His life was here. Here among this crazed debauchery. His lips moved desperately, soft and caring. Tender.

She sighed—a pleasurable sound—into his lips, then with her crossed arms pushed hard against his stomach and away from him. His breath caught in his throat. Her green eyes shimmered up at him, filled with a storm that would come and he could not stop.

She set her chin and turned away, clutching the now-wrinkled linen to her stomach. "Leave me be, Adam." The words bounced off the walls of the hall and into his soul as she walked away.

He closed his eyes and sighed. Stubborn, foolish girl. He shook his head. The master would destroy her. He destroyed everyone's lives he touched.

He opened his eyes, strode along the glass hallway back toward the stairs and glanced down.

The master and his sons still stood on the lawn below, smiling and talking. They had no doubt enjoyed the view he had created for them. He frowned. He wished he had not so publicly dallied with her. They would be eager to bed her now because of it.

Truly capital. He shook his head again.

He needed to place a small deception in their ears to grant Miss Grey additional time to realize she needed to leave. Time for her to escape before she was torn apart from the inside out. He would head to them now before one of them caught her making their bed.

He took the steps down to the main floor two at a time. After turning the corner, he cut through the laundry and out the side door, which led to the lawn and carriage house beyond. This path would place him in their view as if he were simply heading to accomplish more of his day's tasks.

He stepped out onto the stone stair and turned in the direction of the carriage house. Keeping his head down, he strode with purpose. The fresh summer breeze cooled his heated skin, and his stomach pitched, knowing what he was about to do. He loathed lying. He hated even more lying in front of his brother. Why was he doing this for a woman he didn't know?

"Adam," Devlin called from the grass. His rust-colored hair, the same as Adam's and their mother's, glistened in the sun. "Who was the young thing you had so lavishly on display for us?"

Adam slowed and turned toward the men. "She is the new housemaid," he stated from four strides away. No matter how wrong her being here was, he needed to portray himself as he always had. They would see his desire for her if he did not. "Pretty little thing, isn't she?" The hairs on the back of his neck stood in a wave of agitation. She was more than that.

He squared his shoulders and acceded to what was right to do. She needed time. Time it appeared he was willing to risk all he had built here to attain. He stopped before the three men and inclined his head. "My lord, and masters."

Lord Gregor stood to Adam's left, dressed in a pale blue jacket and high-collared shirt, his hat at an angle. He leaned on his carved cane as if bored by the conversation and everything else in life. He didn't bother to acknowledge Adam at all. This was what he wished Miss Grey never to experience.

Indifference from anyone. She deserved better. Just as his mother had.

The eldest son and namesake Christon stood in a light tan coat and striped trousers in the center. He reached up and scratched the hair of his sideburns with his index finger and stared directly at Adam.

Devlin lingered an arm's length from the others, smiling brightly as if nothing of consequence ever deterred him from happiness. For all the indecency that Portage Place was, Adam was grateful for that one small gem. His brother was well. He had grown into a fine and decent young man, despite all the debauchery.

He smiled back at Devlin. Their mother would be happy Adam watched out for him. Somehow, Miss Grey appeared to need him more than Devlin did, now that he was grown.

"From down here, she was a phoenix taking flight," Christon stated, flatly challenging him with his unflinching stare.

Adam turned his gaze on him and fought with himself not to defend her. If he did, he would only draw attention to himself and her.

Christon's green eyes narrowed, cold as the snow on a winter day.

Why was he so upset? Adam smiled back at him without saying a word. Another disagreement with Lord Gregor, no doubt.

"She might prove an interesting fuck later tonight." Christon smiled and his eyebrows rose as he silently waited for more explicit information from Adam.

That smug smile would soon be a fated frown. Adam refused to give more information on the delicacies of Miss Grey. He didn't want to.

Christon rubbed his fingers up the lapel of his light brown linen coat.

He was the one son Adam could not understand and would never wish to be. The next Lord Gregor. He would have much to live up to...or undo when Lord Gregor died. No matter what, Adam needed to respect and answer him. He straightened his shoulders.

"You did an excellent job displaying her for us, Adam, and oh, the sounds..." Christon closed his eyes as if still savoring her delicate crescendo.

The sound of Miss Grey thrashing against the glass as she pleaded her desires crawled unwanted back through Adam's ears and hammered about. His chest tightened. It was a sound...so delightful... He wished it not to leave his memories anytime soon. He wished he alone had heard her. *Do what you came here to do, Adam. Gain her time.* He shook his head in an attempt to dampen the unwanted effects and dispel her voice from his mind.

"Adam?" Devlin said with a cheery smile causing the freckles on his cheeks to squish together. He had their mother's smile, and every time he grinned, Adam thought of her and how she had begged him to watch her poor boy.

Those smiles relieved the twisting tornado of worry that Adam had not done well by their mother in watching his half brother. He would do anything to protect Devlin, including throwing himself fully into the culture of this house, be damned what people thought of him.

Enough. He is happy here. You should be happy then too. Do what you came out here to do, because Miss Grey won't be happy here.

Time to break the eagerness to bed Miss Grey with a crack in the ever-blooming flower of her virginity. He braced himself for the known consequences and slid his hands behind his back.

"One caution, I fret." He frowned and glanced at each of the men. "I tore Miss Grey's cunt. She will require a few days to fully heal." There, it was done. He had not taken her virginity, but he has loosened her. He hoped they would not touch her now. Not for two or three days. "I am sure you saw her tears of pain afterwards."

"Too rough with one who is not yours to be rough with, Adam?" Lord Gregor snapped without hesitation.

Adam slowly turned his attention to him, knowing punishment would be dealt. "My apologies, my lord."

From his shorter stature, Lord Gregor stared up at Adam with dark, punitive eyes that twitched. "She will not be spared her duties, and neither shall you. Hands out."

Adam grimaced.

It is worth it, for her.

His hands would hurt only for a day, maybe two. This act would gain her as many days, he hoped. He slid his hands out in front of him and braced himself.

"Palms up." The master's thick rosewood cane rose into the air.

Adam turned his palms up and steadied his features. The wooden cane with gold inlays whistled down. He exhaled as the rod cracked his palms hard.

He gritted his teeth against the searing pain and slightly narrowed his eyes, but refused to show any weakness. He continued to hold his hands open as the red line rose on his skin. The cane cracked down once more, making a red X on his palm.

"Again, and this time, the backs." Lord Gregor smiled deviously at him, his eyes deepening with an emotion Adam didn't understand. Hatred? Pleasure? Maybe even pain turned in the depths of those obsidian eyes.

Adam flipped his hands knuckles up.

The cane rose back into the dusk sky, then, as if a bolt of lightning slicing the grey, it cracked down on the bones of his knuckles.

Damn. Shit. Bloody hell. He locked his jaw to hold back the stream of blasphemous words ready to bust from his mouth. His head spun and his stomach sickeningly pitched. He concentrated on Lord Gregor's empty eyes.

"Do not *ever* spoil the pleasure for others, Adam. You are a servant of this house. Only I or my sons can have that pleasure." And they had spoilt the pleasure for others. Several times. It was what he feared most for Miss Grey.

"Yes, my lord." His voice held no hint of the pain that throbbed in his hands.

Christon clapped him on the back. "Well done."

"Agreed." Devlin nodded. "I would have been cussing like a dock whore."

Lord Gregor simply turned away toward the house.

"Sir, Lord Norting shall arrive soon," Devlin called to Lord Gregor's back.

Lord Gregor continued on his path. "If we have a new servant, then Doctor Benson is here. I have something to discuss with him." Lord Gregor disappeared into the main parlor doors.

"I couldn't care less if anyone greets Lord Norting or his daughter," Christon grumbled. "I refuse to be made a milk sop simply because he tells me to. This visit won't sway me." Christon turned and walked in the opposite direction of his father, leaving Devlin and Adam standing in the middle of the lawn gawking after him.

"Why is Christon so upset?" Adam watched as he walked out into the fields heading toward the lake.

"Marriage. Father told him he would be betrothed by the week's end."

"Oh. I see."

"The girl Father picked is strictly for appearance. She has good blood and even better estates…I mean manners, of course." Devlin winked, then laughed. "Christon likes his women naughty."

"Indeed, he does." Sibila had been his favorite until recent months. The image of Miss Grey crying in his arms came back to him. A low groan crawled up his throat as an ache pressed in on his chest. Damn Sibila. Damn this house. Miss Grey needed to leave.

"Not all of us are as debauched as the others, Adam."

Adam nodded, barely hearing his brother's words. "I have work to finish." He turned toward the carriage house and strode across the lawn, his hands throbbing.

Christon would wed and nothing would truly change here. Nothing had changed here in the years he had been in service. One small woman would not alter Portage Place and what Lord Gregor had carved. Adam would be damned if he allowed Miss Grey to befall him. He would save her from the hurt and relentless anguish Portage Place caused women of her sweet nature.

CHAPTER 5

The savory smell of duck, thick-crust bread and pudding hung so heavy in the air Emily could taste them. She slid out her tongue and traced her upper lip, gathering the essence that lingered there. Her stomach growled, and she rubbed her fingertips against the carved handle of the large serving tray, waiting for Miss Wicking to fill it for the night's feast. A shiver raced her spine—her fingers wrapped around carvings of nude females.

To her left, the pots bubbled.

To her right, sweet cakes cooled.

Miss Wicking had prepared a feast for the master and his guests. Emily's tray held sliced roast duck cooked to a golden brown. She inhaled and the scent of the sweet, sticky currants and wine, combined with duck, flooded her mouth with hunger. Delicious. She bit her lower lip. If only she were not holding little carvings of nakedness as she stood there. She could almost pretend this was normal and hope some of this night's meal would be left for the servants to taste after the dinner was through.

She rolled her eyes. Other things awaited her after dinner. Things like the tray she held, or worse, the *anything* Mr. Waterton had spoken of. Adam was right. She was a lamb amongst wolves here, but she was gaining experience, and so far he and Sibila had been the only ones to show her anything considered scandalous.

"One more touch, dear Emily. The feast must be as visually seductive as it tastes." Miss Wicking's short, pudgy fingers garnished the tray with sweet candied orange slices.

Emily had not an inkling that she would be serving dinner when she took this post. Then again, she had not known most of what she had experienced today. Serving food required discipline, and she had a terrible habit of watching people. She couldn't help it. People fascinated her.

Leave. Adam's harsh tone from the hall still rang in her ears.

She closed her eyes. *Fortitude, Emily.* She would remain close to Adam. She wanted to know more about him, but until she had a chance to speak to him further, she would remain strong. Concentrating on her chores and doing what she was told was the only way to stop her mind from wandering to the longings those in this house supposedly had.

"Very good, dear. Head up the stairs to the dining hall and follow Mr. Waterton's directions to the letter. You shall make a splendid presentation for my duck." Miss Wicking's ruddy cheeks plumped as she smiled then winked.

Emily bobbed her head and then turned, carrying the heavily laden tray. She traversed the servant's hall and turned into the stair, which twisted narrowly up to the second and third floors.

Adam stood on the landing, staring down at her. The candlelight from a nearby wall sconce played shadows across his face. Her heart flipped and she sucked in a breath. He certainly was handsome. Upon sighting her, he frowned.

He had no cause to be cross with her. She stepped up onto the first of the narrow wood steps, and the tray tilted. The fragrant duck slid to one side.

Adam bounded down the flight of steps and reached to grasp the tray.

Attention, Emily. She lifted her spine. *You do not need his help, no matter how handsome he is. Show him you can survive here so he will not keep trying to send you away.*

Besides, he had assisted her enough today and, even though she had enjoyed her wanton unraveling in the hall— my goodness, she still could not believe she'd done that—he would only continue to fray at her will. "I can manage just fine," she said in a curt tone. Her brows pulled tight.

Adam pulled his hands back and stepped aside to let her pass. "Very well. I need to speak, Miss Grey."

She stepped past him, but remained silent. Gently, she tipped the tray to the opposite side to even out the duck, and with sure footing ascended the stairs to the main level of the home.

He continued up the stairs directly behind her. His heat was so intense and close to her back, her thoughts flooded with the remembered sensations of him pressed to her against the glass as his hands trailed her sides. Her heart sped, and she swallowed hard. *Do not think of such.* She tried to rid the memory from her mind.

"I told you earlier that others would not wait for your permission to diddle you." His breath licked the hairs behind her ear. Oh good Lord. She held in a tremble. "I told the master and his sons that you are not to be touched."

Her eyes widened. He did what? Would that work? Could he simply tell them such and they listened?

H-he'd just told the master she was untouchable. Mr. Waterton's words...*do anything*...splintered as a broken glass in her ears. Oh no! He was daft. She would lose her post.

Emily stopped mid-step and turned slowly toward him. She gripped the carved nude handles as if her life depended on it. The nerve he had to jeopardize her post here! "Pardon?" Sweat dampened her brow. She would be removed from her post before she had any experience, a reference to go by, or money in her pocket. She would be removed before she got to know Adam. She would become worse than what she was here. She would become a beggar or an unfortunate. Her stomach dropped, and she narrowed her eyes at him. "You had no right."

"Miss Grey, you don't belong here. I know what Portage Place is like. You have the three days I granted you before someone demands for your services in the carnal way several times a day. I gave you time to see what this house is truly like...without having to lose your dream on someone else's demand."

He'd gained her time. She tilted her head to the side, and her shoulders softened. It was a nice gesture. More than nice. He showed her he cared about her and wanted to protect her. Her heart fluttered, and her lips curved into a soft smile. They both knew she worked for Lord Gregor, not for Adam.

If the master wanted her, she truly could not stop him, no matter what Adam told them. She stared up into Adam's calm blue eyes and that worry swirled there in their depths. Still, his gesture showed him kind. She inhaled deeply and continued up the stairs, holding the tray. He'd gained her his protection. She bit her lip. She wanted to know Adam even more. "Adam, what did you tell the master?" She reached the top of the stairs.

Adam held open the door into the butler's pantry. Quiet shuffles and mumbles rolled out of the small space as servants scurried about following Mr. Waterton's constantly moving hands. The sound of the evening's dinner festivities rushed down the small galley and over them. Men laughed and chatted loudly. Dinnerware clinked and clattered. Yet little sound came from the activities going on within the butler's space.

"I did nothing to endanger your post," Adam's rich voice whispered as she passed him and pressed into the narrow corridor.

"Miss Grey! The platter. I am waiting!" Mr. Waterton's flat, hushed tone chided from down the narrow room.

"Pardon, sir." Emily entered the room without answering Adam.

Sibila entered from the dining room, a fresh blush on her cheeks and a ceramic pot in her hands.

"Miss Grey!" Mr. Waterton frowned, and Emily rushed forward. "Stand to the left of each person and, using this serving fork, place one piece of duck on each plate. If they request a second piece, please provide it. Do not speak unless spoken directly to. Do you understand, Miss Grey?"

"Yes, sir." Emily bobbed her head to Mr. Waterton and stepped into the dining hall with a quick glance over her shoulder.

Adam still stood in the doorway, watching her. He smiled at her with concern in his eyes. She pushed the image from her mind. She needed to be on her best behavior. Pleasing Mr. Waterton was what mattered at this moment.

She stepped farther into the deep blue dining room as if

stepping back into an older, more animalistic time. The room was dark, with iron chandeliers and red wax candles. Her feet trod slowly on the pale grey-and-red carpet. The pattern brought forth the image of men and women feasting on wild boar, the red juices spilling to a cave floor. She headed toward the long, bulky, immense wood table. Only half the table was set, and only one woman was present.

Emily headed to Lord Gregor, who sat at the head of the half-deserted table. *Do not stare at anyone, Emily. Do not speak. Simply serve. And serve well.* She turned to stand next to him and caught a glimpse of the wall that had been to her back. Her eyes widened. A scandalous painting stretched the entire length of the room. Men and women engaged in all positions of the act were displayed larger than life before her. Emily held in a gasp. Who could eat with that on the wall? *Catch your wit, Emily, the master is watching.*

She stood next to Lord Gregor, fully aware it was the first time she had glimpsed the notorious rogue. She wanted to stare at him. To see what such a scandalous man looked like. Instead, she focused on the delicate floral pattern of the china placing in front of him. Such a stark contrast to the man, the wall and the platter she held.

He reached across the plate, and his hand covered the surface as he picked it up. He raised it into the air. "I agree, gal."

Her gaze jumped to his face. Had he read her thoughts?

He frowned with ice in his eyes. "The wrong plate has been placed before me." He threw the plate across the room. The delicate floral china hit the naughty wall, shattering into tiny pieces.

She flinched, and sweat pooled beneath her cap. What should she do? Run for a new plate? Run from the house? No.

Stay and show fortitude, for this was her reality and she needed to make the best of it.

A new plate appeared calmly over his shoulder from Mr. Waterton. Emily swallowed hard and nodded to Mr. Waterton, who nodded his approval back at her.

Lord Gregor said not another word and turned his attention back to his guests.

She carefully lifted one piece of duck and placed it over the etching of a nude woman in the center of the plain white plate. There, now everything matched. She hesitated a moment to see if he asked for more duck or anything else, then moved to the place setting to the left of him.

From the corner of her eye, she glanced back, catching the square jaw of Lord Gregor. His lustful, heavy-lidded eyes met hers. He sniffed the air and mouthed, *"Your cunt"*, then licked his lip.

A chill raced along Emily's skin, and she bristled, but forced herself to lower her gaze. Had she imagined that? She could not imagine him touching her in any of the ways that Adam had. No matter how refined his education or fat his pocketbook, he simply was not attractive to her.

She turned her gaze to the gentleman seated next to Lord Gregor and let out a small breath. With silvering hair the color of wolf fur, this man appeared older than Lord Gregor and pleasantly subdued. She glanced at his face. His downturned lips and puffy eyes made him appear as if he were a dwarf who had toiled his youth away in search of gold he never found. *What are you doing, Emily? Lower your eyes.* This task was proving difficult for her, simply because she wanted to stare.

"I am sure you will agree the shipments coming in from the east are decreasing in quality—" He closed his eyes and moaned.

How odd. She stepped around him and, as she lifted a piece of duck from her tray, he shifted slightly in his seat and groaned deeply. Seated under the table in front of this man was a dog licking his crotch. Her eyes widened and her hand trembled as she placed a piece of duck on his plate. Monstrous. *You saw nothing. Nothing. Move on to the next plate.*

"One more, girl," he said with thin pouty lips as his hand reached under the table and stroked his dog.

The hairs on her neck stood, and she placed another piece of the fragrant duck onto his placing. "Not for me. For my dog." She glanced down to see that a plate was set on the carpet to the side of his chair.

There was something deeply wrong with a man who allowed a dog to do that. Even more wrong to allow it at the dinner table.

She placed a piece of duck on the dog's plate and moved quickly on. Glancing beneath the table at the next man's legs, she checked to see if he too had hidden pleasures going on while he talked and ate. No one resided at his feet, but his hand rested peacefully upon the flap to his trousers.

She placed a piece upon his plate, then moved to the only woman seated at the table. A woman about her age with black hair pinned so severely back from her face it stretched her eyes thin. The eldest son, Christon, would marry this woman. *Don't stare at her, Emily...* But she couldn't stop. Dressed in a striking, deep candy pink dress, she simply was out of place sitting here in this house. The woman turned in her direction and stared up at her with eyes so black she swore they were devoid of all emotion.

Emily's arm swayed as she set the duck on her placing. Was she serving the devil herself? It wouldn't surprise her here in this home, and why couldn't the devil be a woman?

The lady reached out and grasped Emily's wrist with icicles. Emily flinched. "You are new here and they have given me that dreadful other maid. I wish you to attend me."

Emily's eyes widened, and she bobbed her head. Did she refer to Sibila? She must. Sibila and she were the only housemaids. That would teach her to stare at any person here. She scooted around the back of the woman's chair. In doing so, she caught a glimpse of the scandalous painting once more. The woman focused back on her place setting and did not look up at anyone.

With her tray half-empty, she continued half-seeing down the opposite side of the table as she served the remaining dinner guests.

Over the next hour, she and three other servants served and cleared five courses, which consisted of the small pieces of duck in orange currant sauce, pork cutlets done with lemon, wine and leek, mutton haunch, orange jelly with cheesecakes and a soufflé of rice. They were now to serve sweets.

Adam reappeared in the small serving room along with several other female servants whom Emily had never seen before. Each one of them was beautiful in her own way. It appeared not only were the servants here checked for their health, but that they were required to be visually appealing in some manner. Dessert for the eyes as the sweets went down. Dessert for more than eyes, she guessed.

They would serve a sugar cake decorated with small swirls of candied lemon rind and a fruit ice. Tea and port would also be offered.

"You will each take your silver tray," Mr. Waterton instructed. "On it you will find the desserts you will be serving, along with a long piece of black cloth. Enter the room in the order you are now and stand behind one of the dinner guests. Adam, please serve Miss Button."

Emily's brows pulled tight. That severe woman was Miss *Button*? Miss Button brought forth images of fuzzy rabbits and fancy embroidery. Neither of which were what that woman represented.

Sibila stood beside Emily with only a half-smile. She turned toward Emily, her eyes glimmering with the anguish of tears. "Switch places with me, Emily."

Emily glanced down the small room to Mr. Waterton, then back at Sibila.

Sibila's gaze moved along the men in the dining room, and her voice dropped to a whimpered mumble. "Enough threatening my heart." She rolled her eyes, shook her head and stared at Adam. "Will you?" Her tone returned to normal as if she had quietly confessed nothing at all.

"Surely, Sibila." Emily stepped to the side and glanced at each of the men in the dining hall as she took Sibila's place. Had she referred to Adam with that mumbled comment about her heart? Maybe she and Adam were more than simply friends who futtered. Or had she made that remark about one of the men in the hall? They were all handsome in their own way, but all an impossible match for a maid. Poor thing indeed if she longed for more from one of them, for this house was far from a fairytale or a magical den where a prince would come to sweep her off her feet no matter the social implications.

"So who shall be your first, dear Emily?" Sibila's blue eyes glinted as she questioned her. "You should give the eldest son, Christon, a thought. He is gentle and wicked. It is why I asked you to trade places. So you can serve him."

Emily glanced down the row of servants. Adam stood two people away, his red hair glittering with golden highlights in the candle glow. His gaze settled on Emily with a fire burning deep in his eyes.

Her knees weakened and her throat tightened. He was a lion. A lion that wanted to slowly lick her with his big, prickly tongue. The hairs on her arm stood, and the flesh he had so thoroughly enlivened tingled. In a single line, they followed Mr. Waterton into the dining hall.

"This is a special treat that we like to share with those who are close friends." The eldest son's deep voice pulled her attention to the table before her.

Each servant stepped forward and stood behind one of the chairs. Sibila stood to her right and behind the son whose sheets she had soiled. To Emily's left, Adam stood behind the dark-haired devil woman with the fuzzy bunny name.

His heat unwantedly reached out for her, surrounding her in comfort and unease. Her stomach flipped. It was as if he touched her, though he was an elbow's length away.

Emily stared at the crisp, stiff collar of the eldest son before her. She closed her eyes.

The eldest son reached up and rang a small dinner bell. On that signal, each of the servants raised a long thin slip of cloth up and over each of the diners' heads and slid it across their eyes. Emily's hands trembled as she did the same. Wrapping the cloth about Christon's eyes, she slid the cloth above his ears and then tied it behind his head, trying not to catch his perfectly placed coal black hair.

"Now we are all at the will of our senses and our cocks. If you have one." Christon's deep, commanding voice echoed in the room. "The servants behind you are here to serve you. Take liberties as they feed you. We all do."

Emily leaned around and grasped a small piece of the sugar cake. "Open your mouth please, sir."

He opened it. She brought the cake up to his mouth and he closed his lips just as it touched them. The cake smeared against his closed mouth.

She pulled the cake back. Why had he done that? "Pardon, sir."

"Lean in farther and press your breast against my neck. Clean my lips with your tongue."

Oh dear Lord. Her stomach tightened. So it began. Emily glanced at Sibila as Sibila rubbed her breasts against the middle son Albert's back and with her free hand gently caressed his cheek and chin.

Adam's foot brushed against her skirts, and she gazed at him, catching his eye. His lips curved up, and he leaned in and gently took a spoonful of ice and touched Miss Button's pouty lower lip. She opened and stuck out her tongue.

"Are you listening, girl?" the deep voice called from in front of her.

Emily jumped and turned her attention to the son before her. "Yes, sir."

"Do you understand me?" His tone was harsh and commanding.

"Yes, sir."

Placing her small bosom up on the chair's edge as Sibila had done, she leaned in—her heart pounded so loud in her ears she could hear nothing else—and gently cleaned his lips with her tongue. That was not so bad, and the sweet cake was delicious.

He slid his tongue out and wrapped his about hers, pulling a small crumb into his mouth. Startled, she jerked back. She had not expected that, though she supposed she should have. She inhaled a deep breath and raised the glass of wine. There was a tug at her skirts, and the man before her slowly gathered the fabric of her skirt. Slipping his hand below the hem, he trailed his fingers along her calf. She jumped.

"You are skittish, aren't you? Such a treat." He moved his hand back and forth, caressing her stockinged leg. "Wine, please, and use your mouth."

Use her mouth? She once again glanced to Adam, who now caressed Miss Button's shoulder lightly as he dipped his finger into the glass of Madeira and raised it to her lips.

Emily continued to bring the glass up to the eldest son's lips, and at the same time she trailed the fingers of her opposite hand along his chin to tilt his head back.

Adam bent his knee and pushed harder into her skirts, finding purchase on her thigh. At that same moment, Sibila's elbow gently brushed her upper arm, bumping her and tipping the glass she held. The ruby red liquid traveled up the side of the glass to the rim, spilling a droplet down the outside edge. She would end up dismissed if she spilled the wine, or it would end up being removed from her pay. She glanced first to Sibila. Why had she done that? Sibila's fingers trailed down the jacket of the man before her to the flap of his trousers as if she had done nothing. Emily then glanced to Adam, who glared at Sibila as if she had committed something far worse than sin. Emily frowned.

"New girl." The eldest son before her shifted in his seat. "Either there is something of some scandal going on and you are watching, or you have decided this is not a post for you."

Emily jumped. *Don't lose your post here! Be bold. Adam is watching you.* She brought the glass to her lips, sucked in a generous swallow of the spicy wine and placed her lips to Christon's plush, masculine ones. She imagined she kissed Adam. He parted his lips and she slowly, playfully, drizzled the wine onto his tongue.

He swallowed and swallowed.

When her mouth was empty, she licked his lips, wishing it had been Adam. She wanted to kiss him again to show him how much she appreciated his protection.

"What a treat indeed. Better than a tongue and naughty." His finger traveled up her thigh while at the same time he reached out his other hand for Sibila's skirts.

Emily lowered the glass back to the table and smiled. She could do this. Her breath heaved. It was odd to serve in this manner, but her only other option was to leave. She didn't want to do that yet—

"Ummm." His tongue slid out and glided along his top lip as if searching for more. "You are a taunt."

She hesitated as the tip of his fingers puckered the cotton at the slit of her knickers.

He leaned to his right, reaching out. He grasped and lifted Sibila's skirts. His hand greedily searched for her mound.

Sibila pulled away from him and continued to feed the son before her. The eldest son pushed to his feet, knocking Emily back. She caught her balance and stared at him as in a quick motion he grabbed Sibila about the hips. He spun her to the table and yanked up her skirts. Sibila was silent. He hastily undid his trousers and pushed her legs apart. His manhood stood straight out from him. "Don't you ever pull away from me. Do you understand?"

Sibila continued to stare at him without saying a word.

He thrust his cock into her opening, rattling the dishes on the table. Sibila gasped and bit her lower lip as if enjoying and fighting the pleasure. He thrust again and again.

Lord Gregor reached up and pulled off his eye cloth. "Well done, lad." He then pulled the blonde servant who served him into his lap and grasped her breast. Emily stood frozen, her gaze jumping from one person to the next.

"You indecent excuse..." Miss Button's voice screeched from besides Emily. A glass clattered to the floor.

Adam jumped back and to the side, away from Miss Button's chair. "Pardon, ma'am. I thought that would please you."

"Well it did not!" Miss Button pushed to her feet, ripped the cloth from her eyes. Her eyes widened and she stared directly at Christon, his hips continuing to flex and relax as he futtered Sibila on the table they had just eaten upon. "This family...and this house..." She darted past the row of chairs as if leaving the pits of hell and bustled out of the room.

"I guess she really doesn't like cock after all," Lord Gregor's tone humored from down the table.

Adam stood staring at Miss Button's empty chair as if in shock. He reached out and grasped the glass from the floor, then picked up the remainder of the dessert plates, placing each one on the tray. Not saying a word, he headed back to the small servants' room off the dining hall.

What had happened? Was Adam well?

"This should stop, Christon," the middle son's harsh voice scolded from beside her. His chocolate-colored eyes grew small and beady with disgust.

"No. It should not, Albert." Christon didn't bother to take his blindfold off or even turn his head in his brother's direction. He grasped at Sibila's breast and, with his other hand, reached out and back toward Emily. Instinctively, Emily jumped back a step, out of his reach. Then she closed her eyes. She should not have done that. She opened her eyes to see if anyone watched her. No one did. Her shoulders relaxed.

Albert pushed back his chair and stood. "Well, I will have no part of you ruining a decent woman's mind."

"Carry on." Christon's hand rose into the air and he dismissed his brother with a single flip of his fingers.

Emily slowly scooted to the side, gathered up the remaining dessert items from Albert's placing and headed back into the servant's room as quickly as possible. The room was empty. Where had Adam gone? And what had he done that had so upset Miss Button? She quietly scraped the remaining dessert off the plates and then stacked them to carry down to the kitchen.

CHAPTER 6

*a*dam sat at the large servants' table. Several other servants sat eating and drinking in groups about the long table. He lifted his third glass of red wine to his lips. Serving dinner had not gone well. He normally enjoyed the above-stairs games, but tonight had been stressful and distracting, not to mention vexing. He swished the wine around in his mouth and swallowed, not tasting the fruity essence.

Miss Grey's frown while serving dinner and the dulling of her eyes spoke of challenge and disappointment. He would not change his interference, both with her post and with her task at the table, but he wished she understood his intentions were pure.

Or did that matter?

She seemed set on staying...for the moment. He had given her the time to see what she needed. Then one of the master's sons would take her after those days were up, and his intentions would be useless. No matter the outcome, she would not thank him. She saw his gesture as interference, that much he knew.

Miss Grey entered the room, casting sunshine on his wine-fogged mind. Her hazel gaze, as splendid as a drop of dew on the morning grass, moved with purpose down the left side of the table, then the right. She settled on him staring at her in fascination. Damn, he'd had too much wine. He smiled at her as his heart thumped beneath his breastbone. He liked her. Worse, he feared for her happiness. He would have to explain his failure in the dining hall to her. Miss Button was filled with contradictions. He sighed. Explaining that was not something he wished to do.

The empty seat next to him was the only one at the table. She walked down the right side of the table between the chairs and the stone kitchen wall. She stopped next to him. He did not raise his gaze to her, but concentrated on the glass of wine in his hand.

The air about him smelled of sweet roses. He wanted to inhale again and again, until his nose brushed the soft petals of her skin. His stomach sank, and he closed his eyes, holding in a sigh. Where had such a thought come from? There was nothing more than protection guiding his attention to her. Her good smell was simply a welcome addition.

He opened his eyes as the chair next to him dragged a dotted heartbeat on the floor. *Simply ask her how her first day weighed on her. Nothing more is necessary. You know that. You certainly don't need to explain your actions to her.*

Her lips were thin and as dreary as a dead twig on the forest floor. She sat, and her skirts brushed his legs in pin-picks of awareness. His throat tightened and he cleared it.

"How are you, Miss Grey?"

She stared at him. "Adam." She lowered her gaze as if she

had something uncomfortable to say. "I-I need to apologize…" her eyes met his again, "…for my rude behavior in the stairway and at serving. You did what you did out of kindness, not out of anything more sinister, and I let my vexation with myself out at you."

Adam tilted his head and regarded her as she continued to stare at him as if a expecting a meaningful reply. One that, if he was not floating in a haze of wine, he would probably have for her.

"Thank you." So, he expressed his thanks to her for being kind in the face of such emotional upheaval? He ran his hand through his hair, and the room spun lightly. The wine and the day had truly gone to his head.

He placed the glass back firmly on the table and released the spirit to the rest in the room for their enjoyment.

Her small hand reached out and touched his wrist. "What happened to your hands?" Her soft and soothing tone lapped against his skin as her fingertip trailed up his rough skin to the red welts and bruises on his knuckles.

"The cane," he said flatly while nodding.

"Cane?" Her eyes widened with understanding. She picked up his hand and gently flipped it to show his palms. The bright red welts cut across the center as if they were his own palm lines.

Her pearl-white teeth snagged the plush contour of her rose-colored lower lip. "Oh Adam." Her fingers gently traced the line and then began to rub the uninjured flesh of his palm. Pain mixed with pleasure rippled up his arm, and he did not know whether to shudder or sigh in relief.

Her small, lily-colored fingers continued to calmly draw small circles all around his hands, drawing the ache from a hard day's work and the pain from the cane out to the tips.

With a pinch of her fingers, the strain released into the air that tightened between them. His muscles relaxed and the fine hairs on his neck rose as awareness of her grew.

"No one has ever done this for me." With that one sentence, the deep meaning of the words collided in him. He adored her gentle nature mixed with her spirited streak. "You remind me of my mother." In all the best ways.

She tilted her head up and smiled at him, pleasure showing on her round face. A deep contentment bloomed in his chest as he watched her expression change to one of enjoyment. Her strength showed in this moment. In her sure and untainted caring for others' pleasure. Did she even know it?

A laugh across the table pulled his attention to Miss Wicking feeding the gamesman Goodchild cheese from between her breasts. He stared back at Miss Grey's delicate hands rubbing his churlish palm so tenderly. This house would ruin her by taking and never giving back.

"Why are you still here?"

"I have no other post, Adam. It is either this post and a chance at a reference, or becoming one of London's vast unfortunate pinch-bricks."

Was this post better? He slid out his tongue and wet his lower lip. He could give back to her in a way Portage Place never could. He typically didn't withhold pleasure from his diddles, but he could make it explicit with her.

He would protect her and give her pleasure.

The air about them swirled with the scent of sweat, arousal and lavender. He turned his head. Sibila stood behind them. He nodded slightly to her as his jaw tensed. What she did at dinner would have cost Miss Grey a lashing if she had spilled the glass of wine. He would have words with Sibila for her behavior tonight. Miss Grey glanced at Sibila and smiled a welcoming smile. He would not allow anyone to know his new course with Miss Grey. Sibila would snip Miss Grey's emotions in two if he openly showed Miss Grey preference.

Sibila pulled out the chair across from them and sat facing them. She grasped his cup of wine and raised it into the air. She called loudly, "To Emily. For surviving her first day in sin."

"Here! Here!" Everyone in the room cheered, shattering the calm moment they had shared, and raised their glasses.

Miss Grey smiled shyly and slowly released his hand, her touch retreating to her lap beneath the table's edge. The contentment of her touch wrenched away from him.

That damn word, *sin*.

Damn Sibila for the games she played. He would not play her game this night. She would find her entertainment elsewhere and not at Miss Grey's expense.

He reached for Miss Grey's hand like a puppy deprived, searching for his scratch under the table's edge. His fingers glided over the soft material of her skirts to her arm and her hand lying like a cup waiting for him to fill.

He lazily dipped his fingers down the curved handle of her thumb and into the creased bowl of her palm. Slowly, he drew small, intimate circles on the skin.

She trembled, and he imagined seeing the ripples pooling sin in the teacup of her hand. His gaze stayed steady on her face, blocking out the sounds of the others and of Sibila, who no doubt focused on them.

The soft, creamy skin of Miss Grey's cheek tipped in a rose flush from arousal. Her eyes met his, and her desire burrowed inside his skin. He squirmed, her need wrapping about him. The fear of his touch no longer glared back at him. Lust and true want of him—of *his* touch—was all that resided in her eyes.

The expression alone satisfied his longing desires. He had not seen that heartfelt look on a woman's face since before he arrived at Portage Place. He would not let this moment pass untutored.

"Emily—" He paused. Adam slowly gathered up the velvet material of her skirt and petticoat. He wanted to touch the soft folds of her glistening wet cunt and make her shudder again and again as she deserved. "Pull up your skirts and expose your curls for me."

His throat spasmed. He wanted his cock buried deep in the slick walls of her virgin cunt. He needed to be the one she chose. It could be no other. His brows pulled tight, and an unfamiliar emotion fluttered his gut. His mouth dried as the fear of what that meant crawled up his spine. He wanted more than to simply protect her. He could not deny that.

Take a breath, Adam. She will leave eventually with her reference. Until then... Slow your time and savor her like a lion savors his catch for days.

Emily's eyelids lowered, as if somehow not seeing him made this act acceptable to her. She slowly moved her hands to the sides of her thighs and gathered up her skirts, pulling them up to pool in her lap.

Adam slid his chair smoothly back from the table and to the side so that he faced her.

Her eyes fluttered open at his movement, and she stared at the large bulge in his lap.

He reached out and tugged on her chair, scraping it along the floor as if it, too, resisted this moment, but wanted it all the same.

She faced him, knees to knees. The ivory white of her stockinged legs and doorknob-shaped kneecaps brushed against his. Emily's lashes closed over her deep, longing eyes, blocking off the intensity she so openly showed in them. She would do what he asked because she wanted him.

A smile curved his lips. She was delicious. "Pull it higher, Miss Grey. Show me how damp those curls are."

She wiggled her bottom and at the same time lifted the material up the soft flesh of her thighs to the dark brown curls of her cunny mound.

"Slide your thighs apart. I want to see your lips through the slit in your drawers." He studied her face as her teeth grabbed the soft flesh of her lower lip as if it gave her fortitude.

Her thighs slid silently apart, and she trembled.

What a good girl. His smile broadened and he leaned in. His calm breath mingled with her jagged puffs. "You are delightful, Miss Grey." Soft, petal-red colored her cheeks as if his words were a brush and he the artist of her desire.

"I want to pleasure you now, Miss Grey." His fingers busily worked on the buttons to his pants, and he pulled the flap back, knowing full well what she would assume he meant with those words.

Settling back in his chair, he shifted his hips and pulled the fabric down until it caught where it tucked into his boots. His bare bottom pressed against the hard wood of the chair, and his cock stood straight from his curls.

At the sound of his motions, Miss Grey's gaze swung to his cock, one thought clearly visible in her eyes: his cock in her hands.

He simply needed to get her to feel safe enough with him to make the step on her own. For now, he would do all else to titillate her.

"I will not take you until you ask, Miss Grey. I want to feel your wet cunt on my bare thigh. Stand up. Take off your skirts and straddle my leg."

Miss Grey glanced with hesitation around the room. She swallowed hard. Adam didn't take his gaze off of her. "Miss Grey."

She pushed to her feet, her skirts falling in a swoosh back down her legs and against his. Her hands trembled as her thin fingers rushed to unbutton the skirt from her waist. The material fell, and she stood in a sea of brown waves. He raised his hand slowly as he did when soothing a skittish mare. His fingers touched her still-covered hip. Her aroused heat sucked at his fingers, pulling his mind deeper into her desire.

"Touch me as you straddle me…anywhere you wish." He gently squeezed the flesh and bone of her hip. Fisting the thin cotton lawn of her petticoat in his other hand, he yanked.

The button gave way with a *pop*.

She gasped and stared down at his hand wrapped about the cottony white. Her hands moved as if to cover her drawers in embarrassment. He narrowed his eyes at her, and she stilled them.

He grinned. Damn, he loved that reaction. Innocence, perfection and shock all in one. He unfurled his fingers, and the garment fell into the rippling fabric of her skirt, creating foam on the crest of the brown waves he would teach her to swim upon. His cock pulsed and his throat tightened.

She stepped toward him clad only in her drawers. Grasping his shoulders, she lifted her slender right leg and stepped over his left bare thigh. Her alabaster skin next to his pale leg blended in a blur, joining them in his mind. *Enough, Adam, the wine has you spouting horrid poetry in your head!* He shook his head to rid the wine-induced sappy image and trailed his fingers up the outside of her legs to her waist.

Her chest labored in and out, struggling against her stays.

Pinching the tape to her drawers, she pulled. In an

unraveling of cotton, the front of the garment fell open, exposing her glossy cinnamon curls and blooming lips below. Her flesh quivered beneath his touch.

"Mmmmm." He slid his left hand onto the bare skin of her hip and steadied her as his right fingers splayed across the smooth, flat skin of her alabaster stomach.

The cane lines that marked his hand and the roughness of his work-torn skin shone a drastic contrast. She was unsullied. He was sin. He flexed his fingers in her pureness as if doing so sanctified him.

Inching lower, he closed his eyes to savor the coarseness of her hair. The springy curls scrolled around his fingertips and snaked a deep yearning up his arm that writhed down his spine to his bollocks. He increased the pressure of his touch, needing to hear her voice, her breath, any sound of her pleasure. He dipped his fingers down the slit at her apex.

The humidness of her folds licked at his fingertips, begging him to play, feed and lose himself in her divineness. He tapped his finger once against the slick skin of her opening.

Her breath hitched, and what was left of the room completely faded away on her inspiration.

This frail, beautiful bird of a woman he held captured in the palm of his hand. In this moment, she mattered and no one else.

He curled his finger, gently stroking the outside of her oiled folds. She arched her head back and whimpered, thighs quivering against his.

A thrill raced down his neck and pulled, twitching his cock. "Mmmm." He pushed down on her hip, urging her to sit on his hand and thigh.

She did without a word. Her fingers dug tightly into his shoulder.

"Remember what I told you in the hall, Miss Grey?" Her eyes fluttered open. The black centers huge with arousal, they shone like pools of ebony water at night. "Miss Grey."

"Yes... Tone," she said in a husky voice that plucked the strings on the back of his neck.

"Good." He pulled his hand completely from her watering cunt and laid it on his thigh between them. "Rock your hips back and forth."

Her hips moved, and the wetness of her opening smooshed against his thigh.

God, she was wet, as any wanton dove he had taken in this house...but this was different. She was different. Or was it the wine?

He closed his eyes and simply listened to the sounds of her breath hitch with each rock of her hips. The hard garnet of her sex smeared along his skin.

He reached for her hips, wanting contact with her. She moaned and pressed down. The opening of her cunt suctioned against his thigh as if trying to devour his flesh. Or was it his sanity?

His eyes fluttered open to find her head tossed back, lost in pure bliss as her primal need for pleasure took her. Her mouth open, she moaned deep, loud and long.

Adam licked his lips and took in every detail of her in rapture. Her slit-open lips. Her flared nostrils. The arch of her neck, and the way her back bowed as he tightened his grip on her hips.

Her chest heaved. Her hands flinched and released, then regrasped his shoulders for purchase. Her white belly glimmered with the perspiration of her effort. The heat on his leg grew maddening. He stared at the glistening sheen as she slid back. He groaned. His cock, purple-red, ached to be his leg.

Hands wrapped about his cock hard, and sensation exploded through his bottom cheeks. He glanced down to see Sibila crouched beneath the table. Her hands glided up his cock to the tip. She smiled a harpy's smile.

He stiffened, wanting to tell her to leave him alone, that this moment was all about Miss Grey.

Miss Grey whimpered and placed her head against his shoulder. She rocked her hips, more determined to find release. The last thing he wanted was to break her focus by drawing attention to Sibila's presence.

Sibila's fingers clutched his sack, and she rolled his marbles around in the skin. Her lips came down on his crown.

Oh…damn! He clenched his teeth and thrust his hips up into her warm and wet mouth. He moaned, and he dug his fingers into Miss Grey's hipbone harshly.

Sibila sucked his cock deep into her depths. His hips rocked up and up… Closing his eyes, he imagined his prick popping into Miss Grey's hole. He lost control. The rhythm of Miss Grey's dance ground against his nerves in a delightful procession. His cock slipped in and out of Sibila's mouth, waltzing the same tune.

Sibila's tongue circled his crown and then sucked him deep.

Miss Grey's body quivered, and she cried out as her body jerked and jerked against him. She clutched him as if her life depended on his solidity. Her hot breath puffed in humid bliss against his neck. She stilled against him.

Sibila's head bobbed up and down faster, her lips popping up over his crown as her tongue lapped at him. His sac tightened and his legs jerked, nearing the bliss that would come in a downfall. He wrapped his arms around Miss Grey, molding her upper body to his.

Miss Grey's lips kissed his neck and her tongue licked up to his ear.

Sparks shot down to his sac, and he splintered in erotic delight. He cried out, his sac pulsing his seed deep into Sibila's throat.

Miss Grey sucked his earlobe into her mouth, then licked up to the cup. She laid her head on his shoulder, and her fingers gently played with the fabric at the back of his collar. Miss Grey rooted her nose into his neck, and her mouth moved. The unspoken words, "Thank you", pressed to his skin and slid up between them.

Her apology to him. His to her. Sibila and the others in the room simply disappeared.

CHAPTER 7

*E*mily pulled her head from Adam's shoulder. She'd never felt so relaxed and peaceful in all her life. Something had happened here in this room. Something she was afraid to admit. Adam had touched her in a more intimate, non-futtering way that tugged at her heart. Adam. The man would surely hurt her. He futtered every woman here. Yet there was something…something so familiar about what had happened this night.

She gazed at him, taking in his weary face. She wanted to kiss him. And why not? She had already done so much more.

She leaned in and pressed her lips to his. His lips parted and eagerly moved in strong presses against hers. She moaned into him. Their tongues touched and then his swept into her mouth and twined, tasting of wine. He stole her breath. She gently sucked his lower lip into her mouth and pinched the plump flesh between her teeth. He growled. She released his lip and thrust her tongue into his moistness, then flicked the smooth surface of his teeth. Her head spun. She'd enjoyed what she'd just experienced, though this was so much more. She wanted only him. There was no doubt now.

She pulled her lips from his. "Adam."

He slipped out his tongue and wet his lips as if savoring that taste of her moisture. "Yes, Miss Grey."

"I want more. More with you." Heat crept up her body. She had actually said the words aloud.

His lips turned up and he chuckled. "All right." His green eyes met hers, and her stomach flipped.

She smiled back. "It was silly of me to say."

"No…" His hand rose and tugged a loose strand of her hair, sending pinpricks straight down to her pulsing flesh. "I want more too."

Her shoulders relaxed. He settled his hand on her thighs. She traced the valleys between his fingers, rubbing where they pressed together. She wanted to know more about him, about the little things that were so seldom shared, but she needed to start someplace more broad. "How did you come to work here at Portage Place?" She lazily continued to trace his fingers.

He tilted his head to the side, and the emotion in his eyes slid behind a cloud of uncertainty. He cast his gaze down to her fingers tracing his on her right thigh. "I have always loved working with animals. My mother knew the master, so this seemed a natural fit."

"Did you know about how the house was before you came here?"

"No. I had a false understanding based on gossip and rumor, but the reality was more than what I'd heard." His brow pinched, causing her stomach to churn with unease. "At first I felt free here. Now those same freedoms cage me." His deep emerald eyes stared up at her with an intensity that seared straight to her gut. "This place is my home now. I cannot change that. Though I do miss…little things." His fingers clenched on her thigh. "Genuine caring and touching. No one cares here."

Emily frowned at the sadness in his voice. She would care for him. Had already begun to. Maybe, just maybe, they could offer each other something in this mad house. Something that could grow.

A yawn burst passed her lips, and she giggled.

Those more intense conversations would have to wait for another day. Exhaustion anchored deep in her bones. "Time to retire, I fear. It has been a long day." She glanced around the room at the others engaged in intimate caresses and whispers.

"I know." He held out his hand to her as if helping her from a carriage instead of his thigh.

Her fingers wrapped about his, and she pushed to standing on shaking legs. "Until tomorrow." She pulled up her drawers and tied them about her waist, then bent and scooped up her skirts.

Adam wiggled his hips, pulled up his trousers and buttoned them. "Tomorrow will be just as trying as today, Miss Grey. Get your rest and put something in front of your door." He grasped her about the waist once more and pulled her to him. He kissed her corseted waist and turned his head to the side. His ruddy hair brushed in long stokes to the undersides of her bust. She fingered the short strands.

"Go, Miss Grey. Before I turn total dog and decide to be indecent." He pulled his head from her and dropped his hands from her waist.

"Sleep well, Adam." She left him sitting in the same chair she had ridden him to oblivion on and walked down the length of the dining table and out into the kitchen. She stared out into the dark servant's hall. She would surely trip up the steps if she didn't have a candle. Spinning back on her boot heel, she took two steps toward the dining hall.

"Truly, Adam." Sibila's voice rang heavy.

"Don't, Sibila." Adam's tone was hard.

They sounded like two lovers quarreling, voices filled with emotion and angst. She stilled, pressed her back up against the kitchen wall, and strained to make out the impassioned words.

"Be a pleasure tonight, Adam. Don't bore me."

"What do you think you know about me? Nothing. You know not one whit."

"I know more than you think, and I know how you have the ability to make a woman forget herself for awhile."

Adam was silent, then sucked in his breath as if in pleasure.

Sibila laughed. "See? I shall get my peace before I sleep."

There was another long pause.

"No. I won't. She means…something to me."

Sibila laughed. "I do so adore you, but you know of nothing but what this house holds for you. I do know more… and you will use those good hands on more than just the beasts."

Adam laughed a strained laugh. Or was that genuine? A chill raced Emily's spine. Had Sibila and Adam once been in love? Were they still? Emily turned silently back away from the kitchen without her candle and felt her way along the wall to the stairway.

Deep inside, her stomach pinched. They were lovers. She had been a part of that today in the barn.

She swallowed a lump in her throat. No. Some great

emotion in their words twisted in her in a most uncomfortable way. What was it?

She frowned and ascended the stairs in blackness that mirrored her inner turmoil. She cared for Adam. She had fallen for him from the moment she saw him. He had shown her his inner self, and she respected his protection of her. Yet Sibila... Sibila had also shown her nothing but kindness. How did she fit into something they shared here at this house?

She shook her head. She couldn't fathom them sharing anything beyond futter. But she wanted more. More than empty pleasure. She wanted what Adam had alluded to in the dining hall.

Caring.

Love.

She reached the top of the stairs. One man. One woman.

Would Adam and Sibila be doing the act in her room later tonight? She sighed. She was one too many women. Sleep would elude her with that going on beside her. She would have to do as Adam suggested. Block the door, or...

Hours later, Emily rolled over in the dark and floated in the soft cushion of her mattress. She reached out and found no one in bed besides her. Sibila had yet to return from doing whatever it was she was about. Until she did, Emily could not block the door. Emily rolled back onto her side, closed her eyes and drifted off to a blissful dream of her as the heroine in one of the penny sheets and Adam as the handsome hero who whisked her off her feet and into wedded passionate bliss.

. . .

The mattress beside her depressed, and warm skin pressed to her side. Her nightdress fluttered up her stomach to expose her hips and breasts, then pooled about her neck. How had that happened? She moved her hands to pull the cotton cloth back down, but she could not move them. They were held by a large male hand to the mattress. Her eyes shot open. Ink black resided around her.

"It is too bad you can't be touched. I am quite in need, and Sibila seems to have disappeared."

Whose voice was that? Her eyes widened and her heart pounded in her ears. She bit her lip. *Please let me be dreaming...* She lay absolutely still. He shifted his leg over the top of her left one and pulled, dragging her legs apart. The short, furry hairs on his leg rasped against her skin. She shifted. He ground his stiff erection against her thigh. Gracious. He meant to diddle her.

"I know you are awake."

Stay still, Emily. She swallowed and held her breath anyway.

"I do believe I shall have you use your mouth to ease me. Or..." He gripped her hip and rolled her onto her side. His finger slid between the globes of her bottom cheeks and then pressed against her bum hole. "Here."

It had to be a dream. For who would want to diddle her there?

His finger pressed into her bottom, and she squirmed and pulled her hips away from him.

"Try to relax your muscles. It will hurt otherwise." His finger pressed in. "I am sure Adam was fooling, but does that hurt your tear?"

She bit her lip as his thigh pressed her legs, pinning her in the position. Goosepins raced along her skin, and she trembled.

"Ah… No… Not at all, I see." He wiggled his finger and slipped farther into the star of her bottom.

Her muscles contracted against him as her body turned hot and cold all at once. His teeth bit down on her shoulder.

Creak.

A board on the wooden flood squeaked. He released her shoulder and turned his head toward the noise. "It is about time. Where have you been?"

"I didn't realize I had an appointed time." Adam's deep voice echoed in the blackness as if it were a fire casting warmth on a cold night.

"I thought you were Sibila."

"No, I am not. I came to check on Miss Grey. I had hoped to find her sleeping." His voice was firm and angry.

Adam was here. Her skin heated, and a tingling bloomed through the flesh between her thighs.

"Not likely. I need to be eased, and Sibila is nowhere to be found."

There was a long pause.

He slowly pulled his finger out of her bottom. Her muscles twitched as the tip popped out of the muscled ring. How odd that him placing his finger in her bottom and removing it gave her some form of strange awareness. Or was it simply because Adam was here? She swallowed hard.

"If it is Sibila you seek, she can be found." Adam's words rang flat. Yet every word trailed her skin like the finest silk. Her nipples tingled to hard points.

"I am already here and I am not about to go chasing any woman about the house."

Adam ignored him. "Miss Grey, are you well?"

"Don't be a bore, Adam." He tapped up her hip to her stomach.

"All the same. Miss Grey, are you well?"

The other man's fingers reached her breast, and he gently traced the full swell of her curves. Tingles seeped into the flesh, and she arched, pressing her breast more fully into the contact. She could not help her body's response. It was shameful. It was wanton. In her mind, it was Adam who touched her. Adam who made her respond this way.

"She is quite well, Adam."

"I wish to hear her words, Christon."

It was the master's eldest. The one who was to wed Miss Button. The one who had futtered Sibila on the table at dinner.

She needed to let Adam know she was well. "I—"

Christon's hand that held her wrist released and slid to cover her mouth. "I do not wish her to say a word, Adam. If you want to join me, you may. But don't attempt to tell me what to do. Even in the attempt to find out how this *servant* is."

Adam's footfalls fell on the wood of her bedchamber. "Make room, Christon. I came to check on Miss Grey and I am not leaving until I have done so."

Emily's heart jumped into her throat. What happened from here? Her hands trembled. Adam would protect her. He had taken the cane for her already. If this was part of her duty, she wanted him to be there. She was not ready for another man to touch her, but simply having him in the room made her body respond, and if he touched her too, she could survive this encounter. She could. She would. She would be fine.

Christon shifted on the mattress and Adam sat on the edge. Fabric rustled and boots hit the floor.

"Bloody hell, Adam. Did I say this was a comfort spend?"

"Damn well is, Christon." Adam crawled over the top of them both and laid his large frame between her and the wall.

Emily shifted, and Christon's hand slid from her mouth.

Adam's warm breath heated her ear. "All will be well. Do what you saw Sibila do to me in the barn."

She could not speak. The image of Sibila on the floor of the stall sucking on Adam's long, sleek prick flashed to her mind. She would put Christon's—

She swallowed hard. What would that taste like? Her tongue slid out and traced her lips. She would find out. Adam's soft lips touched hers. Gently, they moved against her mouth. His tongue traced the outer contour, then lingered at the center. Her heart leapt, and she sighed, sliding her tongue into his mouth.

Christon shifted his hands to her breasts, pinching and massaging. Her hands, now free of Christon's hold, fisted into Adam's shirt, seeking his body's warmth, his reassurance. She wanted him and no one else. She would do as he told her was best. He would not let anything of consequence happen to her.

One of Christon's hands released and slid down her back to his cock. His hands jerked against her, gripping himself. His lips came down on her shoulder, and he slid the tip of his cock into the crack of her bottom. His warm, wet tongue fluttered and traced the curve of her shoulder and his teeth bit.

Her lips broke from Adam's. "Ouch!" Her inner muscles clenched. Adam's mouth traced her ear and tingles shot up to her breasts. "I will keep our promise," he whispered. "But I must act as if I know your body carnally. Nod if you understand."

She nodded slowly.

Christon flexed his hips forward, the tip of his cock sliding along her crack and between her legs. He moaned and thrust his hips harder.

"Now up on your knees." Adam's breath warmed her skin. "Mouth to Christon."

"Capital, Adam. So good of you to remember your place in my pleasure."

Adam gritted his teeth so hard they ground against her ear. Adam slid his hand down her arm and gently guided her up. He turned her body so his chest pressed to her back. He grasped her long, braided hair and, as Christon laid down flat on the mattress before her, Adam coiled the long strands about his palm. His other hand trailed slowly from her shoulder down her spine, painting her back in a caring sensation.

She trembled, arching her bottom toward him. He was so firm yet gentle with her. She wanted him. Wanted him to truly take her.

Adam pulled her hair taut. Pinpricks caressed her scalp and trembled down her body. He gently released the tension, and her head instinctively dropped to Christon's lap. Christon continued to stroke his length. He released his cock and reached for her breast once again. Emily licked her lips, then, with her tongue still out, trailed her saliva along the tip of Christon's round head. She flicked the tip under the ridge, gathering his tangy and salty essence. Her lips rounded the top and she hesitated. What did she do now?

Christon thrust up before she could move. His cock slid into her wet mouth, hard and firm, then it drew out and disappeared. She thrust out her tongue and tried to regain her awareness. Adam twisted the hair in his grasp, sending pinpricks down her spine. Before she could adjust, Christon thrust his hips up, his cock catching her slightly parted mouth, and slid inside.

Adam twisted her hair again, lifting her head up and down, not allowing Christon to slide too hastily into her mouth and down her throat. She relaxed. He even protected her in this act. She wanted to bring him pleasure. To please him as she now pleased Christon with her mouth.

"Use your tongue more," Christon ground out in frustration.

She flicked the tip of her tongue at the ridge each time he slipped past her lips and into her wetness. This was not so bad.

"Oh yeah. Oh oh! Lick my bollocks. Now!" Christon fisted his hands into the coverlet on the mattress.

Gliding her tongue down the length of his shaft, she fluttered it into the hairs of his balls. What was she to do with all this hair? She pulled her head back slightly and flicked her tongue through the short, coarse strands in search of his skin.

"Now!"

Adam grasped her hip. Heat seeped deep down to her bones. He clenched her hair harder and rubbed his hips against her bare bottom. The length of his phallus extended against her soft skin and hung heavy between her thighs. She concentrated on the long stiffness so close to joining them together, and her nether lips dampened uncontrollably. She swallowed as he dropped her head down onto Christon's sac.

She sucked the loose flesh into her lips and pulled the balls into her mouth. Adam pulled her head back. Her tongue glided up Christon's smooth skin. Adam adjusted his hips and his cock glided along her dewed lips, the crown parting her hairs. Pleasure coiled through her belly and she moaned deep and loud. Adam's thighs trembled behind her. She wanted him inside her, stretching her wide as his hands had done in the hall against the window. Christon pushed his hips off the bed, and his cock touched the back of her throat.

She gagged.

"That's it, love. Just like that. Such a lovely sound."

She was not Christon's love. Christon could not love anyone but himself.

Adam pulled the soft silk of her hair, twisting it more tightly around his hand. He had not wanted Christon to take control. *Keep your thoughts on her, not on the pulsing need gripping your cock.* He gritted his teeth. The heat from her cunt smothered his weeping hardness as he slid forward again between her legs.

She squirmed against him, rubbing her slick wetness on his hot skin. Damn, waves of tingles contracted his sac. He wanted inside her, but not with Christon in the room. Not with any of the masters around. He needed to be who he always was with them. Not who he wanted to be with her. She needed him, and he would not disappoint her. He had already done that once. He did not want her tears again. Not because he introduced her to this place. Christon simply needed to be sucked until he shattered so he could forget for one fleeting moment who he was and what he had become. He would do and say anything to obtain that.

Adam would prove his servitude with Miss Grey's mouth. He would do all he could to keep Christon's prick away from her other blissful places. She shifted her hips as her head went down on Christon's cock once more. Her thighs squeezed his length, and the scent of rose soap and her arousal trickled up between them. Adam moaned. Why did her scent alone send waves of heat pulsing through him?

He could spend simply sliding back and forth between her thighs with her scent in the air. If Christon could achieve his euphoria and leave the room, he could tell Miss Grey... He could tell Miss Grey...

He shook his head. No. She needed to leave here, and his promise to his mother made it impossible for him to go with her.

Dash it. He wished he could see her face—Miss Grey's lips flaring open with each lowering of Adam's hand and the thrust of Christon hips. Her saliva drooling down Christon's length. Her expression...

He squeezed his eyes shut. Did she enjoy this? Of course she did. The smell of her arousal was pushing his need. But did she enjoy pleasuring Christon? He rocked his hips from right to left into the lushness of her bottom, and her body trembled against him. He pulled her hair and Christon's tip popped out of her mouth with a sloppy sound.

"That's it, love. I am so close. Do that again!" Christon said, heavy with passion.

The dog. His stomach clenched. Get this done so he could...could... Bloody hell. So he could futter her thighs? He clenched his teeth. Not likely. He lowered her hair back down.

Her back arched, pushing her bottom against him, parting her thighs, begging him with her body to continue stroking against her. The heat and wetness of her cunt lapped at his cockhead.

He thrust his cock hard between her thighs and away from her loving hole. She squirmed in protest, and jabbed her hips back harder.

He let his hand down, and she continued to lick and suck Christon's peg, as her fingers wrapped about Adam's cock between her legs.

He jumped at the tender yet unsure touch. He dropped her head back down. She placed the tip of his weeping cockhead at her opening. Oh God. The slickness gripped him, and his sac pulsed. Without hesitating, she pushed back, and he pulled away. No he would not take her like this. She deserved more. But oh! Pricks of pleasure waved through his buttocks, and he shuddered with delight. He wanted her.

"Oh frig me," Christon choked out, and the bed rattled with the power of his imminent release. Damn him, he would not, could not, allow Christon to seed her in any way. Not while she wanted Adam to have her virginity. She pushed back against his groin again. Her wet, swollen flesh glided down the top of his cock with little resistance. He rocked back and forth, his cockhead rubbing her bud. She cried out.

"Oh yes!" Christon yelled. Adam yanked her hair up quickly, her head following. He slid his hand around her stomach and wrapped her back against him and as far away from Christon as the wall would allow.

Christon spilled his seed onto the sheets. "Fuck, Adam."

"Oh!" Miss Grey's body stiffened against his heaving chest. Her body shivered as he remained completely hard, poking out between her thighs.

At that moment, Adam didn't care to think more on what Christon would do to him. All he knew was that Christon had spent, and not in her. Or on her. She was now in his arms and he would take her alone.

The bed jostled. "We will have words, Adam."

"Not now. Now is mine." Adam wrapped his arms more protectively about her.

Christon's knuckles slammed against Adam's cheek, his opposite cheek pressed into Miss Grey's ear. "Nothing is ever yours, Adam. I am too tired tonight to give you a proper punishment, but tomorrow you will meet with the tip of my whip for this." He turned and walked from the room.

Adam held her tight to his body. His cheek pounded. *Just capital. Say you can't leave, then jeopardize your position. Just capital.*

The heat of Miss Grey's soft skin folded around him. He gently laid them down on the mattress and pulled the blanket up over them. Miss Grey trembled but said not a word. His cock radiated inside the grip of her thighs. He kissed her cheek and slowly slid back, his prick impossibly hard. He pushed back through her legs. Sparks of pleasure wrapped his balls tight.

Adam placed one leg over her thigh, caging her in a protective embrace. He licked her neck. Damn, she tasted of salt and sweet peas. He pinched her nipples. "By God, Emily."

She shuddered against him, her elbow rubbing up his ribs.

"Reach down with your fingers and touch us. Feel how wet you are."

Her fingers fluttered against their wetness, then pressed to his cock where it ground against her bud. "Oh!" She pushed her fingertip just inside herself.

His buttocks clenched and the crown of his cock swelled. She was incredible. He couldn't stop, he needed to spend. He thrust forward hard. Turning her shoulder, he pressed her down into the mattress for a better angle.

She arched her back and thrust her hips back into him. Her cunny gaped against his hard flesh. He wanted inside her, but now he needed to spend.

He couldn't stop. She felt so good. He needed this.

Needed her.

He slipped in and out hard of her thighs. Her slick flesh pulsed against the ridge of his head. Pressure rose in his sac.

She was so delicious. His head fogged and pops of light flashed behind his eyelids. "Ahhh." He leaned in and bit her shoulder. She cried out and her cunny leaked more onto his staff. His sack pulsed and his seed spurted hard. He shook, and his cock throbbed again. He had no more. He slid his hand back under her arm and clutched her to him. The room grew quiet. Her heartbeat around him. Through him. *Why? Why?* "Why?"

"I want it to be you." She tilted her head down and kissed the knuckles of his hand wrapped about her breast.

A warm haze of contentment wrapped about him. She wanted it to be him. A smile curved his lips. He wanted that too. "Sleep, Miss Grey. I won't allow anyone else to disturb you."

"Adam." Her voice was but a whisper. "Why are you doing this for me? You threatened your position."

Adam closed his eyes tight. "I am not entirely sure." *No. Tell her.* "Your situation does in some ways remind me of my mother's. She never belonged with the master, but we needed him to survive." He rubbed his face against the back of her soft, plaited hair. "She more than needed him in the end." His mother had loved the twisted rogue and paid for it dearly by taking her own life. He couldn't allow Miss Grey to befall the same end. "Now sleep. Tomorrow will be another trying day."

"Thank you, Adam." Her fingers gripped his forearm and her body relaxed into him.

He inhaled deeply. The smell of her arousal filled his nostrils. *Sleep, Adam, sleep.*

He closed his eyes and her rose scented skin lulled him. The sound of her breathing deepened. His did too. His eyes fluttered, his muscles relaxed and he drifted into the peaceful darkness.

. . .

Creak.

Adam tensed awake. What the bloody hell? He pulled Emily closer to him. His eyes popped open and he stared at the door. *Wake up, Adam.* He wrapped his leg tighter about Emily's thigh.

A faint light drifted closer in the blackness. Someone ascended the stairs. Sibila, most like. His shoulders relaxed.

"Are you certain you will be well? There is no need for you to fret the way you do."

Adam knew that voice anywhere. Devlin. But what was he doing up here?

"You are the only true gentleman in this entire house." Sibila's voice held intimate happiness.

The notes pinched up Adam's spine.

Sibila and Devlin.

His teeth clenched. His only nightmare. Well, not his only one, but bloody hell. His only purpose was to make sure his brother was safe. To protect him. Sibila was more tainted than a gutter dove and twice a shrew.

"You are kind, Sibila." There was a long pause. "Don't let him make you something you are not."

"Thank you again, Devlin. I am in your debt."

Capital. Adam rolled his eyes in the dark and slowly slipped his arm out from under the slumbering Emily. Emily. She was Miss Grey no more.

He pushed up to his elbows and carefully scrambled over her to sit on the side of the bed. He pulled on his shirt and gathered up his trousers. He couldn't allow Sibila to get close to Devlin. The muscles in his shoulders tensed. He had kept them apart for this long. Emily had distracted him.

Sibila appeared in the doorway holding a candle, her hair down in waves of black to her waist. She was a striking woman. If only her heart was as beautiful.

He abruptly stood.

"Did you have a nice night, Adam?" She walked to the washstand and set the candle at its edge.

"Stay away from Devlin." He stared at her. He could not stand the idea of her manipulating him. Hurting him.

She spun about her eyes narrowed. "You cannot tell me what to do, Adam. Serrrrvvvant. You and I are the same. Here for their pleasure. We find solace and peace where we can. You have made your choice." She turned her head and stared at Emily in the dim light. "In doing so, I have made mine."

Adam shook his head. "No. You will leave Devlin be." His throat tightened. "He…"

"I know who he is, Adam. I know all about your mother. I know all about everyone here. I won't do as you say. I never have. Following rules never got me anywhere. Go back to your sweet Emily."

He clenched his teeth and fisted the cloth in his hands so tightly his fingers cramped.

"Leave, Adam. The sun is rising and today is a new day. Leave."

Adam turned from her. *Think, think. You can't allow her to be with Devlin.* He blew out a breath. Damn Sibila. She knew what she was about, but he needed to know more. "What is your wish, Sibila?"

"My wish is something you cannot grant me. Though if you leave Miss Grey alone, I will think about what you can do to make it up to me."

"And you will leave Devlin be."

"Only if you leave her to me. I had a plan, and you are destroying it."

Adam squeezed his eyes shut. Miss Grey or Devlin. He blew out a breath. He would not give either. "We shall see." He walked from the room, his mind lost in the fog of all this house ruined.

"Oh, indeed we shall."

CHAPTER 8

*E*mily awoke to the sound of rustling cloth and the faint light of a single flickering candle on the bed stand. "Time to rise, dear Emily," Sibila said brightly. "Fires need a light and breakfast needs to be served. I shall do the sons' rooms. Please do the guests' rooms and the rooms on the main floor."

She stretched and glanced toward the wall. Adam was gone.

"He left," Sibila said in a casual tone.

Emily turned back to Sibila. "Oh." She pushed herself up onto her elbows.

"Make haste. Lots to accomplish this day, dear Emily." Sibila walked from the room.

Emily sprang from her bed and yanked her livery off the chair where she had folded it the night before. Chores and a reference were why she was here.

She glanced back at the bed. The sheets were rumpled as if two had slept in it. Adam. She wanted to know him. Never had she imagined doing what she did here in this house. But

Adam... He filled her dreams. A man who would protect her. A man who made her feel as special as the moon. A grin turned her lips.

She wished she had seen him as he woke this morning. A lion stretching as he awoke from his den. Bed-tussled hair and that sleepy expression. The faint candlelight flickering against the arch of his brows as his eyes danced with that light and mischief which seemed to always reside there.

She walked to the washbasin. If he were part of her encounters here, she could survive. Last night proved that. After splashing water on her face, she turned back to the bed, grasped a piece of cloth and wiped the cool water from her skin. But what of Sibila? Her words were vague about this place and she thrust Emily into of all this without truly giving her something to anchor to. Well, beyond Adam.

Grabbing the candle on the stand, she walked into the hall and headed down the stairs to gather coal for the fires. She stepped into the corridor and walked the wall of windows which led to the master's sons' rooms. She turned her head toward the view.

Bright rays of sun peeked out from the trees as the night became day. In the red dawn light, Adam stood in the middle of the lawn below, facing the house. Christon circled him, a whip outstretched dragging behind him like a snake in his hand. Emily froze.

Adam was to be punished for his actions with her last night. The hit had not been enough. The long switch Christon held in his hand would cut open Adam's skin.

Oh no. She couldn't stop it. She shook her head and her heart sank. It had already happened. Red lash marks cut through his white shirt, and blood stained the edges of the fabric. It had happened.

Her throat closed off and her hand shot to her mouth. She turned and ran for the stairs. He had taken a lashing for her again. On the landing, she glanced out onto the lawn. They were gone. Where did he go? She turned and continued down the rest of the stairs and into the kitchen. Sibila stood by the coal bin, a filled bucket in her hands. "Here, light the fires, then come back down for repast."

Emily stared at the bucket and out the dry laundry door to the carriage house. "I want to find Adam first."

"No. Chores first, Emily. Then fun. Now, make haste. The last thing the master wants is his guests waking to cold rooms."

Adam would be at repast. She could talk to him and comfort him then. She grabbed the bucket handle from Sibila. Sibila picked up an already filled bucket from beside the coal bin. "I will follow."

She turned back toward the hall. Sibila walked close behind her. When she finished, she would seek out Adam at repast and make sure he was well.

Emily entered the kitchen for the early servants' repast. Adam sat in the same seat he had the night before, where she had ridden him to oblivion. Her cheeks heated as the remembered sensations caressed her body. She walked down the table's edge, passing the other servants already eating their meal. His red hair was freshly combed and hung in soft curls about his head. His brown livery and crisp cotton collar set off the fiery tone. He appeared fine, yet he had to be in pain. Her heart beat wildly, and she swallowed hard. He had held her all night. Wrapped in his strong arms, she had drifted to sleep with ease. He made this place tolerable for her, and she made it hell for him. She grasped the wood chair beside him and pulled it out.

"Good day, Adam."

His dew-colored eyes glanced at her, filled with a contradiction from his usual playfulness. Something weighed on him heavily—no doubt the whipping he had received. "Good day, Miss Grey." His long, strong fingers lifted his cup to his lips.

The red welts on the back of his hand had turned a deep blue and yellow. He had done that for her...and today he had taken more lashes. Worse whacks. She wanted to touch his back to soothe him. She stared at his shoulder. The sight of his white shirt cut open and tinged with blood came back to her.

Her throat tightened. His plush lips pressed to the cup rim, and he swallowed a mouthful of coffee. The remembered sensation of his lips on her skin shivered through her. She needed to touch him, to let him know she cared about him and appreciated what he had been doing for her.

"Adam." She reached out and trailed her finger up his forearm to the dark line on his hand. She gently traced the welt, wishing she could take all the pain away with her simple touch. "I wanted to ask you something. Do you have a moment to talk? If not now, later?"

Adam turned toward her. His emerald eyes churned. "To talk?" He shifted in his chair.

The unique scent of the man he was enfolded her. She lowered her gaze from his intense presence as heat bloomed in her belly. Gracious, he smelled good in a way she'd never expected a man to smell.

His eyebrows went up. "What is this about, Miss Grey? Speak now."

"It is about the house and the master. About you, me and Sibila. And—"

He glanced to the left and back to his coffee cup as if the black brew held the answers. "What about the house and the master?" he asked, not looking at her.

Her brow pinched and a chill raised the hairs on her arms. She nervously wet her lips. "I saw you out on the lawn this morning. I-I…I am sorry." She glanced around the room to the other servants eating their first meal of the day. Not one of them cared to acknowledge them, still, she dropped her voice to a whisper. "You have done so much for me here to protect me from Portage Place. You and Sibila both. I—"

Adam's lips turned down. "Be wary." He glanced to Sibila, then back at her. "Do not readily trust Sibila. She is not always forthright."

"Pardon?" That was a peevish thing to say to her when he did not know what Sibila had done for her.

"Simply, she does what she wants and protects only herself." Adam continued to stare into his cup.

Had Adam and Sibila had a disagreement? "I don't believe that, Adam. She has been nothing but kind to me since I arrived."

"Indeed she has." He half laughed and lightly shook his head. "Did she once ask you what you wished?"

"No." But why would she? This was all so odd. Why was he acting this way? Last night, Adam had been sweet and protective, and this morning… She didn't understand. She stared down at her bowl of mush. It had to be the whipping. He was still smarting from it. She would leave him be for a bit. "It is of no consequence, Adam. I-I will figure it out on my own." She stood from her bowl and walked away from Adam, the table and the servants who couldn't have cared one whit about her. She paused in the doorway and glanced back at Adam. He sat with his head tilted down, staring into his coffee.

What had happened after she'd fallen asleep in his arms?

She had never been whipped. Viewing the scene was ghastly even from afar. A black chill washed over her. She turned out the door and into the wet laundry room. She had no idea what the day would bring, but a bad sensation in the pit of her stomach gave warning that the day would not go well.

She wanted to spin back around and go to Adam, to ask him to take off his shirt and let her tend to him. She squeezed her eyes tightly closed. Foolish. He would have said something to her if he had wanted her help.

She opened her eyes and forced herself to work. In the large stone laundry sink, she picked up one of the dirty sheets from the pile and dunked it into hot, steaming water.

Sibila walked by the door in the kitchen. What if Adam was correct about Sibila? She shook her head at the thought. She didn't like that she struggled with whom to trust in her new situation. Sibila was nice, a wanton for sure, but her heart was engaged. Emily's fingers worked in the warm water and she grabbed a bar of soap from the sink's ledge. She rubbed the rose-scented soap against the fabric, then glanced up through the small rectangular window onto the back lawn.

The significant Portage Place lawn. No good happened there. The men had gathered there and watched her against the glass. Adam had been whipped there. That scrap of soil was one of the places that made this house shocking, if such a thing as a lawn could be so.

Across the grass, Dr. Benson strode from the stables and toward the side door that opened to the parlor. His lean figure was draped in a dark puce plaid jacket with brown breeches and brown boots. He carried a long strap in his left hand and his doctor's bag in his right. His words, *I will do all in my power to enlighten and protect you,* rolled through her mind.

He had seemed kind, in a peculiar way. However, no matter how she tried, she still saw a handsome apparition before her. Someone of this world, but a fey. His long legs and polished brown boots slashed through the grass with purpose. She would talk to him.

She glanced behind her into the kitchen. None of the other servants had left the dining hall. She could go after him, at least to express her desire to talk to him more. Indeed, she would. She stepped out into the dry laundry and onto the same red dirt path she had followed Adam down toward the barn. The day was anything but as beautiful as yesterday had been. Dark clouds hung low and heavy with rain, one more certainty that the day could and would spin about. Her boots cut across the dry red dirt, and she turned the corner onto the crisp green lawn. The doctor rounded the edge of the carriage house. Emily followed, keeping her body close to the wood-and-stone structure. The sky darkened and Dr. Benson stood facing her. She flinched and stopped, the tips of their boots touching beneath the long, soft skirt of her livery.

"Miss Grey. May I be of some assistance?" His mint-scented breath warmed her nose, he stood so close.

Her cheeks heated. "I—um. Sir. You had said you would answer questions if I had any."

His lips curled into a smile. "So I did. What may I oblige you with, Miss Grey?" He twisted and dropped his satchel and strap to the ground.

"I have questions, though not about how a man and woman get along. I suppose some might say I am gossip-hunting, which I am sure is not what you meant when you said you would guide me." No. No, it was definitely not what he had meant. *Silly Emily. Don't waste this good man's time.*

She shook her head. "I am sorry, sir. F-forgive me." She turned and stepped toward the house.

The doctor's fingers wrapped tightly about her forearm. "It may not be what I meant, Miss Grey, but I shall do my best to help you settle in here. Please ask anything you wish."

"Anything I wish… All right." She leaned against the side of the barn. "I had no choice when I took this post."

"Most who come here don't. For all, there is a hardship in taking this post. Yet Lord Gregor and Mr. Waterton will provide you with excellent references so long as you follow the rules. No matter how short a time you stay. Most don't realize this. Many stay too long. Some stay until the hurt eats them alive inside and they lose themselves. Do not allow that fate to befall you, Miss Grey. Leave before you twist yourself to fit in here."

Emily's brows pulled tight. "You are not the first to warn me I don't belong here, sir. Thank you for your words. I will heed them." A small smile tipped her lips.

His white-gloved fingers wrapped her hand. "Your question, Miss Grey?"

She nodded. "Can you tell me about Adam and Sibila? Their behavior confuses me. Both appear to be willing to assist me. Yet I feel as if I am stuck in some jest between them, at times."

He glanced over her shoulder. A gust of wind blew around the corner, and pieces of her long hair pulled loose of her pins and up between them. "The rain will come soon." The doctor's blue eyes slowly darkened as if part of the storm. "Men are often seen in different ways to those they care about. My guess is Adam is drawn to you. You are untainted. Pure. But more. You enchant someone as jaded as me." His lips came down softly on hers.

Emily's eyes flew wide, and her hands came up to push him away. This was not what she'd expected.

"Pardon me. That was uncalled for." The doctor stepped back and then was harshly jerked away from her body. Emily blinked and blinked again. Dear God! Adam spun the doctor away from her. Her heart lodged in the throat. Oh no!

"What's this about?" The doctor's words barely left his mouth before Adam's hand whipped through the air and punched him in the chin. The doctor staggered back, then stepped forward and shifted his head to the side as if stretching his chin. He raised his fists. "Are you certain this is what you wish, Adam? I have a pugilism pin from university. If you wish to fight me, I am more than able."

Adam shoved against the doctor's chest. Hard. His lips turned down and the dark sky reflected the anger in his green eyes.

The doctor barely moved. "You obviously wish to fight."

Emily pressed herself up against the barn. Oh, this would never do. She stepped between them. "Adam. Please don't."

Adam stared at the doctor as if he didn't see her in front of him. He refused to acknowledge her.

"Adam. This was not what you think!"

"Tell me, Doctor, what did you find? Was checking her virtue not enough? I know only the finest is good enough to be plucked by these scoundrels. Did you decide you needed to sample the serving offered up this day?"

The doctor's fist flew through the air, and Emily turned away from them, her heart pounding and a sickening sinking in her stomach. No, no, no. This was not what she had wanted.

Not at all. She wanted Adam. And this house…this house was bewitched by the devil.

She ran, not looking back. The clouds cracked and opened in a downpour worthy of Cheshire, not Cornwall. Her feet traveled down the soiled path from the barn, the red mud jumping up to bite at her soul. Tears ran down her face and her heart pinched. Adam couldn't look at her, yet he fought for her?

No. No reference was worth this confusion. She couldn't stay. She couldn't. She would leave and find something else. These theatrics were simply too hard to bear.

The image of Adam's bright red face as his fist cut through the air flashed to her conscience. No. She hated that expression. Disappointment, anger, and the worst…mistrust.

Her heart squeezed tight. She wanted nothing more than to curl up in a ball and shake. She stared about her at the piles of cloth lain about the small space. The laundry needed doing, and that was what she was here for. Not for Adam. Not for Sibila. And certainly not for any of this wretched pain. She would find Sibila and inform her she was leaving. It was the only sensible choice. What she would do when she left, she didn't know, but Portage Place was simply too much for her to bear.

CHAPTER 9

*A*dam stood staring at the doctor. The scoundrel. The master's pet had let his pecker at a woman. *His* woman. How dare he? The rain pelted his coat in dark drops, seeping through to the torn skin on his back.

Miss Grey was...well, she was special and divine. He fisted his hands at chest level. The doctor simply stood. His penetrating blue eyes and pale complexion were now marred with a red patch on his chin. How anyone could find him attractive was beyond him, but everyone did. Especially men.

"Well, Adam. I never saw this coming."

"Indeed, I certainly imagine not, seeing as backgammon is your preference."

The doctor's white left brow rose. "Tsk, tsk Adam. I was not referring to my attraction to Miss Grey. Mind your manners." He pushed out his chest and tilted his head toward him.

"You like women?" Adam's brow pulled tight. He had never once seen him with anyone other than the master in this house.

"Quite. Though that is still not my point."

"What point?"

"You." A wicked grin turned the doctor's lips. "You are in love with her."

"Pardon?" Love? He shook his head.

"Miss Grey." He chuckled. "I had always thought you knew no other emotion than lust..." He waved his hands between the two of them and then touched his chin. "This was a big gesture. A clumsy but honorable gesture."

Adam ran his hand though his hair.

"Do tell, Adam."

The images of Miss Gray flashed to his conscience. Chewing the piece of apple in the laundry the first time he saw her. Her cap all shifted and disheveled after clinging so tightly to him. The sound of her passion as she cried out her release against the window. And her dreams... Love. Marriage. Caring for one man, and him caring for her. Her touch on his hands as she traced his welts. The hairs on his neck stood. The welts stung, but he had not noticed when she'd touched him.

She was tender.

A savior.

His redemption. He needed her. And she needed him.

If that meant love, he could admit those words. His throat tightened and a shiver rippled through him. Love. He needed to make her leave and he would go with her. She deserved so much more than this house. As his mother had. As his brother did. Devlin...

Devlin. His shoulders sagged, and he spun away from the doctor. "Naught will come of it."

"Oh I would not underestimate the power of that emotion. It alone has made entire kingdoms fall." The doctor stood patiently.

Adam turned away and cut back across the lawn to the carriage house door. Rain drenched his livery and hair, but he was warmed through. He swiped his hand across his forehead. Devlin... Miss Grey... His promise to his mother. He would have to leave here and take Miss Grey with him, turning his back on his mother's wish and his brother. His heart leapt and his stomach knotted. Maybe Devlin would come with him.

Last night, he had slept holding her the entire night. When Sibila had entered and woken him, he had known then in his gut what the doctor said just now. He had deep emotions for Emily.

He strode into the barn and down the hallway. The horses gently nickered to him. Until now, these beasts were the ones he showed his affection to. He needed affection from a woman and he wanted that woman to be Miss Grey. He spun about on his booted heel. He needed to find her. To tell her. He knew not what good it would do, but she needed to know, and he needed to tell it. Damn, he wanted to tell the world.

He walked with purposeful strides down the hall to the main courtyard and entry to the kitchen, then stepped out into the thundering rain. A bolt of lightning cracked off in the distance, lighting up the sky. A symbolic bolt. A symbolic storm. His life was about to split wide. His stomach tightened and he turned back into the kitchen. Mrs. Wicking stood over the bread oven and turned toward Adam. "My, you look a fright. What happened to you?"

He glanced down at his attire. Mud was splattered up his pant legs, and his livery hung soaked through.

"I was not mentioning your attire, Adam. Here, dear. Sit, have a little port. You are flush as a cherry."

"Thanks, Mrs. Wicking, but I need more than port to get me

out of this." He needed her. Emily. His beautiful, innocent Emily.

"Oh dear. Did something happen to the master's colt? Or is this about Christon's whip? Do you need tending to?"

He grasped the bottle that Mrs. Wicking had set on the table and, tilting the bottle back, he swallowed one large gulp. Devlin needed to know too. "Thank you, Mrs. Wicking. The colt and I are well enough. I just need to locate Devlin and Miss Grey."

"I have not seen Devlin, though Miss Grey is upstairs, cleaning the pots, I believe."

He nodded and headed out of the kitchen and up to the main floor. He needed to talk to Devlin first and would check the parlor and the library. If he was not there, he would check Devlin's room.

He strode into the third open door on the main floor. The library was dark, but light filtered through the window on the opposite side of the towering shelves. Adam hesitated. He could do this. It was time. Devlin was growing up into a man in his own right. He deserved to know as much as Adam needed to tell.

He traversed the rows of shelving stocked from ceiling to floor with books. Beyond the last rows of shelves, the room opened up to a wall of glass that showed out onto the side of the house and the small pond to the north. He found Devlin seated in one of the deep leather chairs, book in hand. "Devlin."

His brother looked up at him and smiled that same genuine smile of their mother's. "Something amiss, Adam?"

"Unfortunately so." He swallowed a lump that had lodged in his throat.

"Please sit." Devlin lowered his book and uncrossed his long legs.

There was no other way than to simply tell him. "Devlin, I have been working here for five years now. You are now eighteen. I knew your mother."

"You knew Lady Gregor? How so?" Devlin cocked his head to the side.

"No. Not Lady Gregor. Your mother was a servant here. Her name was Betsy." Devlin's smile slowly straightened. "I too am her son, from her marriage to my father. Before your father came into her life."

Devlin's brows went up and he leaned forward in his chair. He still said nothing.

"Your father and she were lovers for some years. Well, more than that, actually. She gave you to the master when you were born because she could not afford to keep you. She could scarcely afford to keep me. She loved Lord Gregor to the day she died, even though his attention had gone elsewhere." Adam swallowed. His mother had killed herself because he'd left her, but Devlin didn't need to know that. Not at this moment. "It is why I am here at Portage Place. When she died, she begged me to watch out for you." Adam licked his lips. "Which is why I obtained a position here. It was her wish."

Devlin turned toward the pond. "I have no idea why you have come up with such lunacy, Adam. I am a legitimate son of Lord Gregor. My mother Lady Gregor sends me letters. If she were not my natural mother, she would have stopped that when she left."

Adam frowned. "I wish I had a painting or drawing of her. If you saw her, you would know instantly you were related."

Maybe it didn't matter if he believed him. Maybe it only mattered that he had done his best to ensure he was well during his adolescence. His throat closed a bit. No. This was not how things should have been.

Devlin turned his gaze back to him. "Do you have more to say?"

"Simply that I had always hoped we could be the brothers our mother had hoped we would become. She loved you. She loved me. She loved Lord Gregor."

"If this is true, I can't and won't acknowledge it. Not to anyone without becoming that bastard. I like you. I hope you understand. I also love Lady Gregor, even if this house was too much for her."

"What about you, Devlin? How are you in this house?"

"I don't mind it here. I am quite comfortable." His smile returned. "Truly. You have nothing to concern yourself about."

That was it. He had said his secret and Devlin had refused to believe. There was little more he could do. He had failed to convince him, but had no evidence beyond his word. He stood and stared into his eyes. "Know that I have always thought of you as my brother, Devlin."

"You are leaving?" Devlin tilted his head to the side.

"Yes."

Devlin nodded again. "That is why you came to me now with this information."

"Yes. I had hoped…"

Devlin reached out and grasped Adams hand, then stood. The same lighthearted smile curved his lips. "Be well in your travels, Adam."

No, he wouldn't have come. He had been a fool to think he would. Even if in his heart Devlin knew it was true, he would never give up his position as Lord Gregor's son. This would be the last he would see his brother for some time. "Thank you, Devlin." He squeezed his hand tighter and then let it go.

Devlin's ever-present sunny smile faltered. "Good day, Adam."

Adam slowly turned. Sadness and a lightness he had not experienced in an age swirled in his gut. He would never know if he had done enough or if what he had done had affected Devlin at all. What he did know was that Devlin would be fine here, and Adam…well, now he was free. Free to make a dream a reality.

CHAPTER 10

*E*mily walked into the master's bedchambers. The windows were open and the sheer under-drapes billowed into the room. Sibila stood on the opposite side of the bed holding a pillow.

"Emily." Her lips turned up. "Help me turn and fluff the master's mat."

Emily strode forward. "Certainly." She needed to tell Sibila she was leaving, after which she would tell Mr. Waterton, and then this entire calamity would be over and she could figure out what to do.

She reached the edge of the mattress and slid her fingers under the edge, gripping the muslin. Sibila grasped the other side. Sibila lifted her side up and Emily pushed hers toward Sibila's side. The mattress fell and flipped back into place with a whoosh of air.

There, work done, now tell her. "Sibila." Emily stared at her from the opposite side of the bed cushion.

Sibila turned and grasped the long handle of the mattress cane to even out the filling. She walked back toward the bed.

"You would be surprised what the master uses this for." The long, thin handle ended in a bent series of circles. She raised the cane into the air and brought the long stick down on the mat directly in front of her. *Thwack!*

Emily jumped. *There is no need to hesitate. Tell her.* "Sibila, I wanted you to be the first I told."

"Oh?" She stepped around the corner of the bed and continued to head toward her, thwacking the cushion as she came.

"Quite so. I have decided that this post is too vexing for me. I am leaving."

Sibila's hand stopped mid-swing on the edge of the corner of the bed. She lowered the cane slowly, never taking her gaze from it as it touched the muslin cover. She jerked her head to meet Emily's gaze.

Goodness, her face was flushed.

"I am sorry you have come to that conclusion. I-I..." She rounded the corner to stand before her. "I am sorry you have come to this conclusion." She raised her arms, threw them around Emily's shoulders and squeezed her.

"Thank you, Sibila. You were very supportive. I—"

Sibila ran her fingers down her arms to her wrists. In one quick motion, her fingers gripped her left wrist and yanked her arm up hard behind her back.

Pain splintered through Emily's arm and her eyes widened. "Ouch."

Sibila's face remained stone and she quickly turned Emily, wrapping her other hand behind her back.

Pain radiated through her biceps. "W-what are you doing?" Emily pulled on her hands, but with each motion pain crippled her upper body movements. She was unable to free her wrists.

Sibila quickly wrapped a length of lace about her wrists behind her back and tugged tightly.

"Sibila? Sibila!" She was not listening.

Sibila slammed her head down hard against the mattress. Emily tried to turn her head to the side, but Sibila climbed up on to her shoulders, pinning her.

Emily twisted and thrashed, kicking out, but found no purchase. Why was she doing this? Was this some jest?

"I am more sorry for this, Emily. You see, today is my last day at Portage Place. And you, you see, have to stay. You are the only way I can leave. I had hoped to present you to him later this afternoon after chores, but this will have to do." Her fingers gripped her hair and yanked her head back out of the mattress.

Emily screamed. No one would come in to help her. Oh dear God. No one.

Sibila's fingers came into view with one of the master's bed sheets. Emily screeched. Sibila forced the sheet into Emily's mouth, tying it tightly behind her head. "There now, you will be quiet as I prepare you for his gift."

His gift? What was she talking about? This was insane. Sibila truly was touched. Emily tried to talk, but the dry, cottony sheets muffled and dried her mouth. It was impossible.

Sibila slid to the side of her. "There."

There was no way Sibila could move her. No way at all. Emily squirmed and kicked out at her, trying to dislodge her, trying to do anything she could to get back on her feet.

"You slick tart." Sibila turned toward her. "Don't bother." She reached for another sheet. Emily's eyes widened as Sibila wrapped her fingers under her arms and pulled her up fully onto the mattress.

Emily continued to kick and wiggle. This was not a jest. Sweat dampened her brow and trickled down her back. Adam was right about Sibila. Sibila was going to do something to her, something totally against her will.

Sibila grasped her hard about the ankles. Emily kicked out, but hit nothing. Sibila grabbed her left ankle and pulled her leg to the large post on the corner of the bed. Emily twisted in the opposite direction, yanking on her leg. With her free foot flailing in the air, one of her kicks landed soundly on Sibila's arm.

"Ouch. Stop that." Sibila pulled a thick piece of leather that was tied about the post and looped it about her ankle. She let her ankle go and, as Emily kicked out, the leather tightened snugly.

There were restraints attached to the bed that tightened as you struggled? Her heart sank and her stomach pitched. She kicked violently at Sibila with her free leg while at the same time attempting to roll her body toward the tied leg and the door. Sibila flung herself across Emily. Weighed down, Emily pulled her free leg up and kneed Sibila in the side.

"Stop that!" Sibila grasped her other flailing ankle.

Oh God, this was not happening!

Sibila yanked, pulling her other leg to the opposite pole. Emily kicked and squirmed, her ankle coming loose from her grasp only to have Sibila recapture it and successfully loop her leg in the harsh restraint.

"Don't you understand? You are the only way. I-I can't stay here any longer. I can't leave him without someone who will pleasure him, care for him. If you leave, I will have to stay. I-I can't."

Emily lay on her back, her hands tied behind her bottom. She was gagged with her legs ripped impossibly far apart by restraints that tightened if she moved. Her skirts lay tangled and her hat askew.

Calm, Emily. Someone will come at some point. She lay motionless. She twisted her shoulders in an attempt to see Sibila.

Sibila appeared above her. She grasped a pillow, folded it and held it to the side of her face. Oh no! She was going to smother her. No! This could not be happening. A tear ran down Sibila's cheek. She wrapped her arm about Emily's waist and lifted her hips, shoving the pillow under her bottom and hands. Emily's breath came quick, and she swallowed against her dry mouth.

Sibila worked with haste as she undid Emily's skirt and pulled the fabric, tearing it from her body. The breeze from the storm outside cooled her skin as she lay with the skirt material torn from her front. The pillow arched her hips into that air. With her legs wide, she could only imagine the humiliating view. Cramps rumbled in her tummy.

Sibila untied her knickers and splayed them. Her fingers trailed up Emily's inner thigh.

"You are beautiful. He will be pleased."

To whom did she refer? The master? Adam? Or one of the sons?

Sibila undid the buttons on the front of Emily's blouse She pushed the fabric open. "This is not how I had wanted to display you for him. But it will have to do."

Emily didn't know what to do. Her heart pounded and she lay there, unable to move.

Sibila knelt beside her and simply stared. Her eyes, blue as sky, were empty, void of emotion as tears slid down her cheeks. It appeared she was in pain and somehow believed what she was doing was her only way to relieve her pain. To her, Emily was her only option. Emily squeezed her eyes shut. She couldn't stare at her. This was not the option Sibila should be pursuing.

Where was Adam? Oh God, he would not come for her. The doctor had kissed her. He had been so angry. He would never come for her.

Sibila ran her fingers along Emily's cheeks. "I am sorry."

She pushed up from the mattress and left the room.

Emily stared at the ceiling. What was going to happen to her? She tried to swallow, but it was impossible. Whomever Sibila brought back to this room would take her as she laid there unable to move, totally exposed. She would not choose the first person to enter her body. Sibila had chosen for her.

She pulled at her legs, and the cool air played along her skin and the place between her thighs. The cotton strip! She had forgotten to place it this morning. Dash it. Her heart sank. Whoever came into this room could get her with child. She squirmed and the leather tightened, spreading her legs a bit farther apart. She should not move. The muscles on her inner thighs stretched and burned. Maybe her hands were the area she should concentrate on. She wiggled them, but the lace bit into her skin and stiffened. They, too, would not budge.

Her fingertips tingled behind her back. She stared at the ceiling and then the curtain billowing into the room. Tears stung her eyes. She should have left when Adam had told her to. She squeezed her eyes tight, pushing the tears down her cheeks and into her hair. She had wanted to stay to get to know Adam. Now she was displayed, the sacrificial virgin for a man she didn't want. Her head grew light and the room spun. *Calm yourself. There is nothing you can do now.* She inhaled a deep breath through her nose.

Concentrate on the sounds in the room. The rain pelted against the window and the window covers flapped in the wind. A clock dinged eight somewhere in the distance. Every sound in the house made her flinch. What if someone unintended came in? A shiver raced up her spine. This was the master's bedchamber. She did not want him touching her. She had wanted to leave this place, but what if the man Sibila offered her to was Adam?

She had craved his touch this morning and wanted more than what this position could offer her. She had thought he had wanted her, but then his behavior at breakfast made her doubt that. Her heart pinched. He didn't want her. He couldn't even look at her after the doctor had kissed her. But if he did come, everything would be well. He would untie her. That truth fluttered deep in her gut. He had always protected her. He would not allow anything of consequence to happen to her. Footsteps came in the hall. Emily stiffened and concentrated on the voices. *Let it be Adam. Please let Sibila have gotten him.*

"This way," Sibila said.

"I am so glad you came to me, Sibila. I-I had begun to think you serious about having nothing to do with me."

"You will see."

The footsteps entered the room. There was a moment of silence. "What is this?"

Emily turned her head to see Christon standing beside Sibila. She closed her eyes.

Christon. She was giving her to Christon. A cold sweat stuck to her neck. Was Sibila in love with Christon?

Christon was to wed Miss Button. Though he certainly would still have a diddle with the servants. He would certainly do the act with Sibila again.

Sibila had said she did this because she needed to leave, but could not do so without offering Christon something?

Her!

My God, she offered her as if she was something that belonged to her. She belonged to no one. She would shortly belong to the streets and be fighting to survive. Christon walked to the bed and stared at Emily tied. He turned toward Sibila. "I-I thought *you* wanted me, Sibila. What is this?"

"A gift."

"A gift? I want you, Sibila. I want you tied like that before me. Don't you understand?"

"You are marrying, Christon. There will be a new mistress of Portage Place. You and I cannot be." Her voice cracked.

Oh no. She was crying.

"And what is this servant supposed to do for me? Take your place?"

"She—she will take care of you. She will show you—you can achieve what we share with another maid."

"No." He shook his head and blew out a breath. "We have more than pleasure between us. Yes, we both find pleasure in others. But—but damn it. I need to know you are always with me. Mine."

Oh my, in his own way Christon loved Sibila too. Emily watched in awe as he fisted his hands and paced back and forth before the bed, agitated.

"I can't, Christon. I won't. Watching you spend your life and have children with another is more than I can bear. I-I am leaving today." Sibila stuck up her chin. "She is your new pleasure." She pointed to the bed. "Take her."

Emily swallowed. They loved each other. He didn't want to dally with her. He wanted Sibila, and only with Sibila would he do as he did. Emily's mind spun. Sibila was naïve to think that anyone could replace another. Love was not interchangeable. If it was, well, it wouldn't be love. Love grabbed hold and would not let go. Love was what made relationships last. Love was what made people do and think crazy things.

Christon stepped toward Sibila and ran his both his hands through his ink-black hair. "I will not wed her." He stepped closer, and refisted his hands at his sides. "I have told Father. The only woman I will wed is you. Miss Button's money be damned. Let Albert wed her." He caged her against the wall, the curtain billowing up behind them.

"Don't," Sibila's voice choked out.

Through the sheers, he grabbed Sibila by her nape and pulled her body up to his, the thin fabric clinging between them. "You make me crazy." He leaned in and kissed her.

Adam stood outside the door that led on to the master's hall. He would tell Emily he was falling in love. No... That would not do. He was in love with her. His heart pounded. He had seen that same love in her every act toward him. He would leave here today with her. They would plan a life. Find work. Live and love together. His uncle had said he always had a place for him at the mill. He would tell her about him.

He would tell her all about his brother, about his promise to his mother, and that no matter what, he wanted her to leave with him today.

Together they would find a way to survive. The doctor had said love was powerful. He wanted to believe that. What he did know was that love, unlike lust, was not denied, and Emily had touched him in a place he had not known... Her hands had led to his heart. Tears and soft caresses. His heart beat faster when she was in the room.

He stepped into the hall and strode with purpose down

toward the bedchamber. He turned into the doorway. Christon pushed Sibila up against the wall and passionately kissed her.

Adam glanced at the large, four-post bed and his mouth dropped open. Emily laid spread wide, gagged and tied. "What is going on here?"

Christon pulled his head back from Sibila's lips. "Be a good lad and take that chit there on the bed, Adam. She is ready for a good fucking, and I have other interests." He yanked on Sibila's skirt and the fabric tore. "Sibila, you are a foolish woman. Strong, smart and foolish." He grabbed her by the shoulders and pulled her into a hug. "Don't ever leave me."

Adam walked to the foot of the bed. "Are you well, Emily?" His stomach knotted. What had they done to her?

She nodded, and a tear ran from the corner of her eye and down her face.

He reached with shaking hands for the gag and untied it. "Are you sure you are well?"

"Quite." She worked her mouth and swallowed. "I was frightened when Sibila attacked me and tied me." She wet her lips "When I realized he did not want me, well, I was relieved." A smile curved her lips. "All I kept thinking of was wanting you to come in and save me."

Who couldn't desire her? "I want you, Emily." He gently traced the lace at the top of her shift and swallowed the lump in his throat. *Tell her, Adam.* He leaned in and pressed a kiss to her lips. "I am in love with you." He leaned back and stared down at her, then smiled. It was the first time since arriving at Portage Place that he had smiled so broadly. Damn, it felt good.

"What?" Happiness, excitement and a bit of disbelief danced in the depths of her eyes.

He still couldn't believe it himself. "I am afraid so." He

nodded and smiled more widely. He was happy. "Never expected it, but I have so much to tell you." He reached her shoulders and gently lifted, sliding his hands down her arm to the binding on her wrists. He gently undid the lace, freeing her hands. He pulled first the left, then the right from beneath her. He slowly rubbed her wrists, her palms and her fingers.

She groaned. "They sting."

"Wiggle them, they will feel better soon." He released her hands.

She wiggled her fingers and laid her palms face down on her corseted stomach. "Adam. I thought you were mad at me. This morning…"

"I was a milksop. I could not admit to my… Honestly, I didn't recognize what was happening until I hit the doctor." He cringed.

She pushed up onto her elbows. His eyes lingered on her outstretched, still-tied legs. "Shall I continue to untie you? Or?" He raised his eyebrows in question.

A pretty pink burned her cheeks. She was adorable and womanly. And his. He didn't want anyone else to have her.

"You are lovely all stretched out for me." He touched his fingertips to her inner thigh.

"Then take me."

He glanced over his shoulder. Christon and Sibila were gone. "Not like this on the master's bed. But I shall, just like this, when we have privacy, you naughty cat." His heart had lifted his spirits. He was giddy.

"Yes."

He reached down and untied her ankles, then picked her up in his arms. Emily giggled and rubbed the side of her face against his shoulder. He squeezed her soft curves to his torso and inhaled the scent of roses. A warm contentedness pulsed through him. This was right. She belonged with him. He turned and walked her from the room. When he reached the stairs, he carried her down to the main floor and out onto the lawn and into the carriage house. He strode past the black-and-brown lacquered coach and into his room, shutting the door with his boot heel. He gently laid her on the unmade bed and sat next to her. She was so beautiful. Her brown-red hair and her lily complexion called to him in a way no other had. The life and happiness that defined her shone in her eyes and lifted his soul.

"Adam. You want me? I want you. Only you." She slid her legs together and glided her fingers about his waist.

His hand splayed across her belly. "Then so be it. We will make our life's work. I will take you away from here and we will make our dreams come true."

"I want that." She pushed up her bottom, arching her body toward him. "Please."

He smiled at her. "Sinful, Emily." He dipped down through her hairs and into her core. Slick, warm lips parted open for him. He fluttered his hand on her mound, watching her intake of breath, and then slid his body over her. The air steamed between them. Parting her legs with his knee, he kneeled between. Her tongue darted out, and she wet her lips. He wanted to join with her. This moment was what they desired. In joining, they would express their lust. In caressing, they would express their love.

He quickly undid the buttons on his breeches. Grabbing his cock in his hand, he leaned in and gently placed the head to her opening. She bit her lip and closed her eyes. "Put your arms, wrists crossed, above your head."

She did so. Her breasts thrust up. Her body extended beneath him. Every curve that was Emily extended for his view. The curve of her neck, the round swell of her breast, to the concave of her waist. He ran his hand down to her corseted hip and slowly slid the tip of his cock into her. Her oiled sheath stretched and popped over his ridge, encasing his head. "Mmmm."

"Oh!" She bit her lip.

"All well, Emily?"

"Quite." Her lips curved up and she arched her hips, sliding farther down his shaft.

He reached up and wrapped her wrists in his hand, then pinned her to the bed. "I have so much to show you. I have lost my heart to you and I want us to achieve your dream. Lust and love and marriage." He pulled his cock to the tip.

"We already have two." She breathed and then arched her hips, sliding back down his length.

"Oh?" He smiled at her. She needed to answer, and he needed to hear she loved him too.

"Quite."

He ground his hips against her, forcing his groin to rub her clit.

Her body trembled and her eyelids fluttered. "Oh! Lust. We definitely have lust."

He pulled out, and her sheath gripped him, sending sparks to his bollocks. "Ah. Quite so. We do indeed have lust." What a lust it was. He would futter her for hours.

She squirmed and wiggled, but he refused to move. Her body shook against him.

"And the second?"

Her eyes focused straight on his.

His stomach fluttered as he waited for the answer.

"Love. We have love, Adam."

His heartbeat controlled his breath. Indeed they did. He

didn't think he could smile any more, yet he seemed to. "Indeed. Lust and love, the two I thought never to mix. They do. And from the start of our relationship, you have had me over the moon for you." He pushed his manhood back into her wet, swollen sheath and groaned.

"Oh?" Emily winked at him. "I have that effect?"

"Well, I can't get enough, I fear." He trailed his fingers down her arm to her hair and curled a loose lock about his fingers. "I am going to love you hard…" he ground his pelvis against her blissful spot, "…and slow." He pulled back at a snail's pace. Her body jerked, and she tossed her head to the side and bit her lip. "And make you scream out your pleasure for the world to hear, but…" he stopped with the ridge of his head spreading her opening wide, "…before I do, I need to know. Will you?" He grinned down at her. She quivered. Oh this was fun.

"Will I?" she whispered, and her eyelids fluttered shut.

"Quite so, Emily. Will you make all our dreams come true? Will you marry me?"

"Adam." Her eyes widened, and she smiled brightly at him. "All three?"

"Yes."

"Oh Adam, yes I will." She pushed up and pressed her lips hungrily to his. "I love you." A tear ran down her cheek.

"You'd better, because I love you too, Emily."

~

PARANORMAL ROMANCE

Sexy Beast IIII

including Lacy's *Kiss of the Dragon*

ABOUT THE AUTHOR

Lacy Danes made a New Year's resolution to write a hot, historical romance. A year and a half later, she achieved her goal. She lives in Seattle, Washington, where besides writing she enjoys horseback riding, gardening and savoring a great martini while watching the world go by.

Visit Lacy at her web site
www.LacyDanes.com.